LOVE AND MISTLETOE

....

A BALLYBEG ROMANCE

(BOOK 4)

ZARA KEANE

Beaverstone Press LLC
Switzerland

To the Romance Divas
for all your support over the past few years.

CHAPTER ONE

....

BALLYBEG, COUNTY CORK, IRELAND

Location: The MacCarthy Farm
Time: 21:06

There were many places Garda Brian Glenn would rather spend his Saturday night. Dry places. Warm places. Places that didn't stink of cow shite. Wrinkling his nose, he hunched down behind a bush and squinted through his police-issue night-vision binoculars. "They've finished unloading the car."

Sergeant Seán Mackey shifted on the grass beside him, the sudden snap of a twig serving as a timely reminder to keep the volume down. "Are you sure about this?" His breath floated through the damp night air in smokelike wisps. "Because if you're not, we're trespassing on private property. Not to mention freezing our balls off. Trust you to pick the first cold night in September to go on a flaming stakeout."

Brian lowered his binoculars and grinned through the dark at his partner and superior officer. "Speak for yourself. I had the good sense to wear thermals. Seriously, man. My intel is solid. The MacCarthys are definitely up to their old tricks. I overheard Sharon discussing it with Naomi Bekele in the pub. Brazen as brass."

4

The police sergeant grumbled and tugged his hat lower, presumably to shield his ears from the harsh wind. *His perfectly flat ears...* Seán was film-star handsome with a deep Dublin baritone that made the women of Ballybeg swoon—a far cry from Brian's sing-song Donegal lilt and sticky-out ears. If his new partner weren't a decent bloke and a fine cop, he'd have resented him.

"Come on, Seán. Sure what else would we be doing this evening? At least a stakeout is more exciting than breaking up a fight at MacCarthy's pub."

"Who are you trying to convince? Me or yourself?"

"This is the first interesting lead I've got on, well, anything in ages. Not much happens in Ballybeg." And when it did, the local police weren't left in charge for long. At the rate Brian's career was going, he'd be stagnating in uniform until retirement. He needed something—anything—to impress the higher-ups.

"I realize Sharon hasn't been the most law-abiding of citizens," Seán said, "but I can't see her manufacturing drugs in her own kitchen."

"Why is it so hard to believe?" Brian forced himself to keep his irritation no louder than a whisper. "You haven't been down here long enough to know the full story about that family. Apart from the father being a regular fixture at Cork Prison, one of the brothers was convicted of drug dealing a couple of years ago, and a second was done for possession."

"Yeah…" The older man drew out the word, giving it a wealth of meaning, "but Sharon's previous infractions include shoplifting, speeding, and drunk and disorderly behavior. And all her priors are at least a couple of years old."

He stared at his partner, slack-jawed. "How the hell do you know all that?"

Seán gave a low chuckle. "The MacCarthy files were among the first to cross my desk when I started working at Ballybeg Garda Station. I've read everything we have on the entire clan, including the fact that Sharon has cleaned up her act since she started university."

"Do you really think attending college has magically transformed her character?" Brian snorted in disgust. "Come off it, man. Think of all the students who are busted for dealing. Being clever enough to get into uni doesn't mean you're smart enough to stay on the right side of the law."

"All right. Don't get your thermals in a twist. We'll check out whatever is going on in the house. I just hope we don't end up making tits of ourselves in the process."

"Apart from not landing face first in cow shite, my main concern is avoiding a close encounter with one of Colm MacCarthy's hellhounds."

"Jaysus. Don't tell me he's still involved with the dog fights?" Seán's mouth curled in disgust. "I knew the judge should have given more than a fine the last time he was up in court. That man's more of an animal than the ones he breeds."

"Agreed. I've nothing concrete about Colm and the dogs, but I could have sworn I heard one bark earlier. Did you hear it?"

"Can't say I did, but it's hard to hear anything over this wind."

Brian hunkered down in the shadows and peered through his binoculars. Shapes moved against lit windows, but he couldn't identify who they were. "Vicious dog or no, we need to get closer to the house. I can't see anything from this distance."

"Me neither. Pity the station's budget can't cover more powerful binoculars."

"The station's budget doesn't cover roof repairs, never mind binoculars," Brian said dryly. "I can't move in my office without tripping over a bucket. It's been like that since I was first sent to Ballybeg. We're always being promised more men, better equipment, and a new station building. It'll never happen."

Seán hung his binoculars around his neck and turned up the collar of his coat. "Come on, then. Let's go."

They crept through the field as silently as they could manage, the house and farm buildings looming closer with each step.

"Wait!" Seán grabbed Brian's arm. "Do they have motion-detector lighting over the yard?"

He considered before answering. "I don't think so. No lights came on while they were unloading the car. Either they'd deliberately switched them off, or they don't exist."

"All right. Go on."

Moving stealthily, they covered the last few meters of the field and took up their position behind an ancient water trough.

Seán rubbed his hands together to keep them warm. "I'm frozen. I'd kill for a cup of coffee right now."

"I've a thermos in my pack." Brian slid his rucksack off his back and extracted a metal can. "It's tea, not coffee."

His partner gave an exaggerated shudder. "How did you make it through training college without having the shite beaten out of you? Everyone knows cops drink coffee."

"Everyone knows cops drink *bad* coffee." Brian unscrewed the top of his thermos and poured piping-hot tea into the lid. It burned his tongue when he took a sip, but he relished the warmth wending its way from his mouth to his stomach. He held the cup out to his partner. "Sure you won't take a swig?"

Brian couldn't see Seán's face clearly in the dark, but he could sense the indecision flickering over his features. "Ah, go on, then. I'm desperate." The other man had the cup halfway to his lips when a sharp bark hacked through the silence. The cup of the thermos shot out of his hand and ricocheted off the metal trough, knocking against a rusty bucket in the process. "Feck." Seán cradled his hand. "I'm after scalding myself."

"That was definitely a dog." Brian craned his neck to see over the trough. Lights went on in the room nearest the back door. A human-shaped shadow flitted across the window. "Someone's coming. Duck."

Voices floated out the open door, the occasional word decipherable. Voices from a house that was likely to be a lot drier and warmer than Brian and Seán's current location. The dog barked again followed by a high-pitched whine. Footsteps rang over the cobblestones, and light from a flashlight bobbed in a drunken dance. A woman wearing high heels. *Sharon.* Brian would bet his police badge he was right.

He pictured her in his mind: medium height, medium build, generous bust, and a high, tight arse that begged to be pinched. *Jaysus.* Where had that notion sprung from? He couldn't stand Sharon MacCarthy. She unnerved him, seemed to take a devilish delight in taunting him at every opportunity. She was no beauty—not in the classical sense—but there was something about her that caused men to look twice. He crouched down and waited for her and the dog to go back inside.

Minutes dragged by. Finally, right at the point Brian was ready to scream from holding still for so long, a door creaked shut, and the clickety-clack of the heels moved back across the cobblestoned yard to the house.

When the lights in the room nearest the back door went out, his tense muscles slackened.

"Whatever eejit of a hound Colm's got now is a useless guard dog," Seán whispered. "Why didn't it pick up our scent?"

Brian shrugged. "Dunno. No sense of smell? Maybe he got it cheap."

"No sense of smell or not, it sounds vicious." Seán shifted restlessly. "We're going to have to try to get a look in the window. Without proof that they're up to something they shouldn't be, we've no business being here."

"You go, and I'll shadow you?"

Seán laughed, a low rumble. "Nice try. This stakeout was *your* idea. *You* get to do the honors."

"Fair enough."

"You can leave the thermos with me."

Brian tossed it to him with a wry smile. "Changed your mind about hating tea?"

"Nah. More like not changed my mind about being cold. At least the can will keep me warm."

After giving the yard a quick scan to check for prowling animals and lurking humans, Brian emerged from behind the trough and half crept, half ran to take up his position beneath a windowsill. Cautiously, he unfurled enough to be able to peer in the glass. The sight that assaulted him was enough to give a man heart failure. A furry face was pressed to the window, lips drawn back to reveal sharp fangs.

***

Location: The MacCarthy Farm
Time: 21:06

Sharon surveyed the ingredients lined up on the kitchen counter: Epsom salts, coarse sea salt, baking soda, corn starch, citric acid, essential oils, and food coloring. Everything they needed to make fabulous homemade bath products. "The Ballybeg Christmas Bazaar won't know what hit it. We'll make a fortune."

Naomi paused in the act of unpacking a selection of cupcake-sized baking molds in a variety of shapes and sizes. "I don't know about making a fortune. Personally, I'd settle for making our money back." She fingered a little bottle of lavender oil. "Did you have to go and spend so much on the ingredients?"

"There's no point in bothering if we're going to use shite ingredients. Decent essential oils don't come cheap." Sharon patted her friend on the back. "Don't stress. Not only will we break even, but we'll make enough profit to afford the rental deposit on a decent-sized flat."

Naomi's expression was dubious. "I certainly hope so. This has wiped out the last of my savings."

"It'll be no problem, Nomes," Sharon said cheerily. "Trust me."

Rummaging through a cupboard, she located the kitchen scales behind a broken toaster and her brother's bong. She stood and stretched her back like a cat. "Hey, if our bath product range takes off, we might persuade a couple of shops in town to stock them. I know Olivia sells stuff like that at the Cottage Café."

"Don't jump the gun." Worry lines creased Naomi's normally smooth forehead. "We haven't made our first batch yet. It might be a disaster."

"Such pessimism! Relax. It'll all be grand. What you need is a large glass of vino before we get to work." She wrenched open the fridge and assessed its contents. Beer, beer, and more beer. Sausages, bacon, and moldy cheese. She extracted a carton of milk and sniffed. *Holy mother.* When had it gone off? A shudder of revulsion ran through her body. Thank God she rarely ate at home. Standards in the MacCarthy household had never been high. Since Ma died, they'd plummeted to a record low.

Grabbing the lone bottle of wine and slamming the fridge door shut, she pivoted on her platform heels and almost tripped over a mobile bundle of fur. "Well, hey there, Wiggly Poo. Did you have a nice snooze?" She bent down to stroke the dog's curly fur. He wagged his tail and gave her a generous lick. "Buttering me up, eh? At least one male in my life loves me enough to kiss me. What's it you're after? Food?"

The labradoodle darted to his bowl and waited, panting and tongue lolling in expectation. Sharon plonked the wine on the counter and rooted through her bag for the tin of dog food that her boss, Bridie Byrne, had given her earlier in the day. She emptied it into the bowl, and the dog consumed the foul-smelling substance with gusto.

Naomi switched the oven on to preheat for the bath bombs. "How long are you dog-sitting?"

"Just for this evening. Bridie's minding him while Fiona and Gavin are off on a romantic weekend, but she didn't want to leave him alone in her house while she was out at bingo. He's a little on the wild side and has a penchant for ornaments."

Naomi laughed. "Sounds like you and he are a matched pair."

"Get away with you." Sharon uncorked the wine and poured two generous glasses. "I've cleaned up my act since Ma got sick. I promised her I'd get my psychology degree, and get it I will." She scrunched up her nose. "Concentrating on my studies would be a whole lot easier if I didn't have to live with Da. The second I can afford a place of my own, I'm out of this dump."

Naomi raised her glass. "Then let's hope the bath product plan bears fruit."

"*Sláinte*." They clinked glasses, and Sharon took a sip of wine, relishing the tart taste on her tongue.

A crash outside in the farmyard made her choke midswig.

"What was that?" she spluttered. She raced to the kitchen window and yanked back the frayed net curtains. Through the dark mist, she could perceive only the pitch black of the night.

Naomi moved to her side, craning to see. "Did one of the cows get out, do you think?"

"Dunno." Sharon was already moving toward the mudroom and the door to the yard. She snagged her jacket from its peg and grabbed her scarf.

"Are you sure you want to go out there alone?" Naomi pulled her cardigan tight around her thin body. "It's creepy when it's this dark."

"I'll be grand. It's probably just one of the animals. Besides," she said with a grin, "I don't see you offering to join me."

Her friend shuddered. "I don't like the dark at the best of times. Out on a farm with wild animals roaming? Nuh-uh."

Sharon laughed. "*Domesticated* animals, you eejit. You'd swear we had lions prowling the property."

"All the same, I'm staying put."

"Suit yourself." Grabbing a flashlight, Sharon ventured out into the dark.

Rain fell in heavy sheets, forcing her to yank up her hood. Up until a couple of months ago, they'd had floodlights that came on when they sensed movement. When they broke, Da hadn't bothered to fix them, insisting a flashlight would suffice and was a hell of a lot cheaper. Sharon shivered in the damp chill air, cursing herself for not wearing a heavier coat.

"Woof!"

She whirled round to see Wiggly Poo slip out the door and dance at her feet. "Daft dog." She petted him and buried her nose in his curly fur. He was a crap guard dog, but she was glad to have his company. Despite her bravado, the dark farmyard was kind of creepy. She shivered beneath her thin jacket. The weird sensation of being watched sent prickles down her spine. If only Da would fix the damn floodlights.

Picking her way carefully over the cobblestones, she headed toward the cowshed. All quiet, save for the odd moo. It was a similar story in the sheep's enclosure and in the henhouse. The familiar sounds and smells were bittersweet. When she was little, they'd had a farm full of animals. Now they were down to six cows, eight sheep, and four hens. Times had changed on the MacCarthy farm, and not for the better.

She closed the door of the henhouse. Whatever had caused the crash wasn't apparent out here. "Come on, Wiggly Poo. Let's get back inside before we're soaked through."

Back in the kitchen, Naomi had started weighing and mixing the ingredients to make bath salts. "No luck?" she asked, raising an eyebrow when Sharon and Wiggly Poo returned from their outside adventure, wet and bedraggled.

"I don't know what caused the noise. The animals all seem fine." She leaned over her friend's shoulder and sniffed the air. "Divine. What scent combo are you making?"

"Lemongrass and lavender. We can add a little purple food dye to give it an appealing color."

"Sounds good. I'll get started on the bath bombs."

"Woof!" Wiggly Poo was on the alert, racing to the window and jumping up to press his paws against the glass. "Woof!"

"What's up with him?" Naomi asked. "I didn't hear anything."

Sharon's shoulders slumped. "Feck. I hope it's not Da. He said he wouldn't be home until late tonight."

The labradoodle was growling now, the menacing sound mitigated by his cute and fluffy appearance.

Naomi's dark eyes widened. "Do you think there's a pervert out there? I told you I thought someone was watching us when we were unloading the car."

"A wanker? He'd need to be seriously desperate to venture out on a night like this." Wiggly Poo was growling at the window. "Oh, for feck's sake." Sharon marched to the window and threw it open.

A pale face loomed before her, light blue eyes darting from side to side, panicked. "You were right, Nomes. It *is* a pervert." Sharon crossed her arms over her bosom and grinned. "Hello, Garda Glenn."

CHAPTER TWO

....

Brian staggered back from the window ledge. His mouth moved but his brain was having trouble connecting with his tongue. The furry mutt, acknowledging him as a nonpredator, morphed from snarling antagonism to drooling delight. Its human companion leaned out of the window, wearing a fuchsia-lipsticked grin and a very low-cut top.

He blinked and tried to focus on anything but her silky-skinned cleavage. "It's Wiggly Poo," he muttered, finding his voice. "I thought—"

"That he was a savage beast terrorizing Ballybeg?" A plucked eyebrow arched above Sharon's sparkly blue eye shadow. "Thank you for your concern, Garda Glenn. It's comforting to know Ballybeg's police force takes its duties so seriously. I'll be sure to tell Bridie to make a poster warning people about the rabid labradoodle who's liable to lick them to death."

Mortification burned a path up his cheeks. "We wondered if your dad was still involved in dog fighting."

The thin eyebrow arched even higher. "We?"

"Evening, Ms. MacCarthy." Seán's voice rang across the yard. He emerged from behind the water trough and strode across the cobblestones with a swagger that Brian would love to emulate. Knowing his luck, any attempt at a swagger would result in him slipping on the slick stones and landing on his arse.

"Sergeant Mackey." A stiffness had entered Sharon's tone. She didn't like Seán. Brian had gotten that vibe off her before but didn't assume her preference for him over his partner was a compliment. More than likely, she took Seán's position as police sergeant seriously, whereas she regarded Brian as a massive joke.

His partner stopped before the window, exuding charm and authority in equal measure. "Garda Glenn and I took a stroll and heard barking. We thought we'd come up and investigate." He flashed an ingratiating smile, but the effect was lost on Sharon.

"No way could you have heard Wiggly Poo from the road. Besides"—she gestured toward Brian's neck —"binoculars? Hello? You two must take me for an eejit."

"Busted," Seán said, nonplussed. "We came up here to check on suspicious activity. Didn't we, Garda Glenn?"

"Like what?" Sharon's gaze roved between them, settling on Brian's still-burning face. "Two women hanging out on a Saturday night?"

"We thought—" Brian caught Seán's warning glance. "Okay, I thought... you and Naomi were talking in the pub about manufacturing product."

Her thickly lashed eyes widened, and her expression turned to granite. "And you assumed that *product* was drugs? Despite me not having any history of drug consumption or dealing, being a MacCarthy is sufficient to have the pair of you sniffing around the farm at night, scaring the crap out of us?"

"Hang on a sec." He wasn't letting her derail his investigation that easily. "You and Naomi *were* discussing ingredients and chemicals. The pair of you clammed up lightning fast when I approached the counter."

She folded her arms across her chest, elevating her impressive breasts even further. "Naomi and I are entitled to have a private conversation without the local constabulary listening in, but if you're curious to know what we're making, you're more than welcome to sample our wares. Go round to the back door, and I'll let you in." With that, she slammed the window shut.

He bounced on the balls of his feet, darting a glance at Seán. "Have I made a major cock-up?"

"Come on," his partner said with a resigned sigh. "We'd better keep her sweet lest she file a complaint with the superintendent."

That was the last thing Brian needed. He'd worked hard to convince the super to approve his college tuition in spite of the tight budget. Pissing the man off now would not be a smart move.

When they rounded the side of the house, light spilled out from the open back door. Sharon stood on the threshold, hands on hips, a sardonic curl to her plump lips. "Come on in, lads. Welcome to our den of iniquity." Catching Brian's look of surprise, she added, "Yes, I have read *Gone with the Wind*, Garda Glenn. I can and do read, shocking though that might be to you, especially given that I work part-time in a *book shop.*"

A book shop he'd accused her of vandalizing only a few months previously... *Damn.* He'd better pray they found something incriminating in the house to warrant tonight's escapade.

He wiped his muddy boots on the doormat and released himself from the confines of his thick scarf. A strange smell wafted through the mudroom, teasing his nostrils. It reminded him of something, but he couldn't pinpoint the source.

"The kitchen's through here." Sharon closed the back door and led them toward a smaller door. "Watch the step on your way down."

When they entered the kitchen, the smell was overpowering. It wasn't unpleasant. Far from it. *But pungent...*

Naomi Bekele was removing a baking tray from the oven, the beads in her hair jangling with her every movement. She froze when she saw them, her mien wary. If Sharon was no more than average-looking, Naomi was a stunner. Light brown skin stretched over high cheekbones, slim-but-shapely figure, and soulful brown eyes. Brian had always felt he should fancy Naomi and was more than a little irritated with himself that he didn't. His gaze slid toward Sharon. She was keeping a tight grip on the labradoodle, which was straining to greet the new visitors.

"He's a crotch sniffer." The trademark cheeky grin slid back into place. "Might be more than poor Garda Glenn can take, especially when he's about to be confronted with the shocking sight of our drug-dealing endeavors."

Naomi's doe eyes grew large. "Our what?"

"Brian here thinks you and I have gone into business as Ballybeg's latest drug dealers." She turned to Brian, catlike. "You don't mind me calling you Brian, do you? You've hauled me down to the station so many times over the years that I feel we're intimately acquainted."

Was it his imagination, or did she place a special emphasis on the word "intimately"? The stab of lust took him unawares. He bit his tongue, remembering all too clearly the humiliation of discovering he'd been wrong to accuse her of trashing the Book Mark last year. He swept an arm toward the stacks of ingredients on the counter. "If you're not manufacturing drugs, what's all this paraphernalia?"

Sharon jerked a thumb at the baking tray. "Bath bombs. Neither an explosive nor a mind-altering substance was used in their creation." Her lips twisted into a sly grin. "You're more than welcome to try one out in the upstairs bath. I promise I won't peek."

He exhaled through his teeth, excising an erotic image of them naked in a bubble bath. "I'll pass, thanks," he said gloomily, seeing his longed-for promotion vanish behind a dark cloud. He'd jumped the gun. Again. Once more, it was over Sharon MacCarthy.

Seán sniffed at a bowl containing small, purple-colored rocks. "What are these crystal things?"

"Bath salts. We're planning to sell them at the Christmas bazaar." Sharon slid an amused look at Brian. "Unless the Ballybeg police force has a reasonable objection to our enterprise."

"We wouldn't dream of objecting." Seán revealed the slow, crinkly-eyed grin that had most of the female population of Ballybeg swooning.

Sharon didn't blink. "Are we done here? Because Naomi and I have bath bombs to bake and wine to consume."

"Sure." Seán straightened and turned toward the exit. "We'll leave you ladies to it. Right, Garda Glenn?"

Brian opened his mouth to respond, but the sound of a car roaring into the yard sent his instincts soaring into high alert. The car door slammed, and someone stomped into the mudroom and toward the kitchen. Beneath the generous application of blusher, Sharon's cheeks paled.

He took a protective step nearer to her. "Who—?"

The door swung open. Colm MacCarthy stood in the frame, wafting whiskey fumes and malevolence in equal measure. His beady, bloodshot eyes took in each of the room's occupants and come to rest on Sharon. "What the fuck are two cops doing in my house?"

"It's grand, Da." All good-natured humor had evaporated from her demeanor. "They thought they saw something suspicious in one of the fields and came up to see if we were okay."

"Something suspicious? What? A stray sheep?" Colm's dark orbs swiveled. "What have you done this time, Sharon? Don't fucking lie to me."

Brian didn't like the way Colm's gaze bore into his daughter, nor the way she flinched under her father's harsh stare. "Nothing." He moved between father and daughter. "She's done absolutely nothing. Sergeant Mackey and I heard barking. We came up to check if you were up to your old tricks. Turns out the dog was Wiggly Poo."

The canine in question growled at Colm and edged his furry arse closer to Sharon. Brian was impressed. The mutt must be smarter than he'd given him credit for.

"Sorry to disturb you on a Saturday night, Ms. MacCarthy." His look was laden with subtext. "I'd love to take you up on your offer of some fresh eggs, though. Will you show me where they are?"

Her facial expression exuded studied indifference but she took the hint. "Sure. I'm sending a few home with Naomi too. We have far more than we can use."

She allowed him to lead her through the mudroom and out into the yard. When they reached the henhouse, he yanked her inside. It was pitch black and stank of poultry. He groped for a light switch and struck gold on his third attempt. "Are you all right?" he asked after light flooded the small building. "I wasn't getting a good vibe off your father."

She focused on the dirt floor, then hit him with the dazzling high-beam effect of her direct gaze. "I'm fine. In any case, I won't be living here much longer, so there's no need for you to be concerned."

"You're leaving Ballybeg?" The notion hit him like a blow to the abdomen. Sharon MacCarthy drove him crazy, but he didn't want her to *leave*. She was part and parcel of his life here.

She gave him an arch look. "Don't get too excited. I hope to leave the farm in a few weeks, but I'll be staying in the area for another few months. Once I get my degree, I'm out of here."

"About the drugs, I might have—"

"Jumped to conclusions?" Sharon crossed her arms under her breasts, recalling his attention to her fabulous cleavage.

He shifted his weight from one foot to the other, feeling like the proverbial village idiot. "I might have made a mistake."

"Indeed?" She unfolded her arms, shoved a few eggs into a cardboard holder, and thrust it at him. "You wouldn't be the first. Everyone around here assumes the worst of me. It's one of the reasons I can't wait to see the back of this provincial dump."

She pivoted on her heel and marched out into the darkness.

He caught up with her by the water trough. Across the yard, Seán was loitering by the house door, waiting for him so they could go home.

"Listen, I'm sorry for disturbing you. And for jumping to conclusions. Best of luck with your bath products."

Sharon turned to face him, and he caught a glimpse of the wry twist to her lips in the moonlight. "Good night, Garda Glenn." She lowered her voice to a sultry whisper. "Watch for wild cows on your way out."

CHAPTER THREE

···

On Monday morning, a blustery wind blew a bleary-eyed Sharon down Patrick Street. She'd used Sunday to catch up on course material from the first two weeks of the semester—weeks she'd spent clearing out the last of Ma's stuff with zero help from her father. Her brother Ruairí had taken care of the admin in the aftermath of their mother's death, but sorting clothes and personal effects had fallen to Sharon.

Neither of her sisters would darken the door of the farm now that Ma was gone. Frankly, she wouldn't either if she had somewhere else to go. However, that was about to change. Once she and Naomi started selling their bath products, she'd have the money to move out of home—and away from Da.

When she reached the Book Mark's familiar turquoise door, she fumbled for the key. Inside the shop, she stumbled to a halt and gasped.

Her boss, Bridie Byrne, leaped up from a chair, half-moon spectacles askew. "You scared the bejaysus out of me. What are you doing here this early? You're not due to start work until nine."

"Yeah, I know." Sharon's book bag slid off her shoulder, forcing her to make a grab for it before it hit the floor. "I wasn't expecting to see you here already."

"Obviously." Bridie was regaining her composure. "Now that we're both here, let's have a cuppa and a catch-up. I barely get a chance to talk to you these days. You're always rushing off to the library."

"I'm late starting my final year at uni. I need to get my arse in gear and hit the books."

"Laudable," Bridie said, "but we can still have that chat. Coffee?"

"Yeah. An espresso would be great."

The older woman filled the kettle with water for her tea and switched on the coffee machine. The latter was a relatively new addition to the Book Mark Café, and a welcome one as far as Sharon was concerned. "I could kiss your niece every time I see that machine. The memory of that instant crap you used to serve still gives me the shudders."

"You, Fiona, and half of Ballybeg have made that perfectly clear, missy," Bridie said dryly. "As for me, I'm sticking with my tea."

Within a few minutes, the hot beverages were prepared. Sharon scooted into a seat at one of the six tables in the bookshop's little café. Bridie lowered her bulk into the chair opposite. She'd recently tinged her iron-grey hair with a purple rinse. Bridie alternated between purple, peach, and pink, adjusting her bright lipstick to suit her current hair color. She didn't give a damn what people thought of her, and anyone who objected got an earful. Sharon totally wanted to be Bridie when she grew up.

"How's life treating you, Miss Sharon? You've been positively quiet lately. Punctual, even. I'm starting to fear for your mental health."

She let out a bark of laughter. "After all the lectures you've given me about embarrassing the customers and coming to work late, you're complaining because I've cleaned up my act?"

Bridie took a sip of her tea and contemplated her employee over the rim of the porcelain cup. "Not complaining. Merely observing. Seriously, Sharon. I know the past few months have been hard for you, and you know I'm not the touchy-feely type. But if you ever need to get something off your chest, I'm here for you."

A lump formed in her throat, painful and resistant. "Thanks, but you know me. I'm a survivor."

"I do know you. I see a forty-years-older version of you every time I look in the mirror. That's *why* I'm concerned."

Sharon toyed with the handle of her espresso cup. Bridie had been great after Ma died. Never asked the usual concern-tinged questions or spouted pat condolences. She'd just given Sharon a reassuring pat on the back and plenty of work to keep her occupied while she muddled through the grief at her own pace.

She released her espresso cup and shifted back in her chair. "I miss Ma but I'm relieved her suffering is over."

"Cancer is an awful disease."

Sharon nodded and took a shuddery breath. "I promised her I'd finish my degree and that's going to be my focus over the next few months. I'll never be as smart as our Ruairí, but I've brains enough to do well in my exams if I knuckle down and study."

"Does this newfound motivation have something to do with you coming into the shop so early?"

Sharon shrugged. "It's quiet here. Peaceful. There's no Da. No pesky siblings. No farm work that I might as well do, seeing as I'm sitting on my arse doing nothing, to paraphrase my father."

Bridie grimaced. "Colm always had a way with words. So you've been using the Book Mark to study?"

"Yeah. I know I should have asked your permission first, but—"

The older woman held up a hand. "It's fine. Provided the shop and café are fit to receive customers when we open, I have no problem with you coming in before your shift."

She released a ragged breath. "Thanks, Bridie. I appreciate it."

"No problem." Her boss stood, her gait awkward. Despite a recent hip operation, she wasn't as spry as she ought to be for a woman in her early sixties. Sharon knew better than to ask her if she were in pain. Bridie got enough of that from her niece, Fiona. Although Sharon had worked alongside Fiona at the Book Mark for several months while the older woman had been ill, they'd never advanced beyond the point of tolerating one another for Bridie's sake.

ZARA KEANE

Sharon cleared their cups and wiped down the table. "By the way, I've ordered a couple of college text books using my staff discount. Hope that's okay."

"It's a perk of the job. What courses are you taking this semester?"

"I need to get the last credits toward my psychology degree, then write my thesis. Starting this week, I'm taking forensic psychology and advanced social policy."

Bridie's jerk to attention sent her glasses sliding down her nose. "Forensic psychology? Interesting. Know anyone else taking that class?"

She shrugged. "I'm sure I'll bump into a few classmates from previous courses." Apart from a couple of coffee buddies, she didn't really have friends at university. Many of them lived on campus or in student digs in Cork City. While she'd attended some social functions, she'd spent the first couple of years of her degree rushing back to Ballybeg the second her classes finished for the day, either to help look after Ma or to work in the Book Mark. That didn't leave much time for leisure. Hell, it hadn't left much time to study, she reflected ruefully, as her mediocre grades from the previous semester could attest. But she would turn it around this year, make her studies her primary focus. She'd never graduate top of her class, but with hard work and concentration, she could push up her average.

Laughter rumbled in Bridie's throat. "I heard a rumor you had a visit out on the farm from Brian Glenn and Seán Mackey."

"Those eejits." Sharon scoffed. "Glenn had the audacity to accuse me and Naomi of making drugs in our kitchen. Drugs! What a plonker. We were practicing making bath products to sell at the Christmas bazaar."

"Aha! So that's what you two were scheming last week. How did your sample wares turn out?"

"Not bad at all, if I do say so myself. We need to adjust the dosage of the essential oils in the bath bombs to get the right amount of scent. Other than that, it was easy peasy." And surprisingly fun. She'd been so preoccupied of late that she'd been neglecting her friends. It had felt good to hang out with Naomi, especially once Da stomped off to the TV room and left them in peace.

"Are you and Naomi still planning to find an apartment to share?"

"Yeah. Hence the bath bomb scheme. We're hoping to save enough for the deposit on a flat plus the first few months' rent. With our part-time jobs, we've both got money coming in each month, but I can't really take on more hours if I want to pass my exams."

"Hmm." Bridie wore a contemplative expression. "Are you set on finding a flat in Cork City, or would Ballybeg do?"

"We're aiming for Ballybeg, actually, at least until the end of the academic year."

"Good to know. One of the tenants upstairs wants to sublet his flat for six months, starting after Christmas. If you and Naomi can cobble some cash together between now and then, the flat's yours. It would only be until next summer, but it would see you through your final exams."

Sharon's stomach gave an excited leap. "Are you serious?"

"I wouldn't have said it if I wasn't. Talk it over with Naomi and get back to me."

"Will do. I'll mention it to her this evening." She'd seen the flats above the Book Mark. They weren't large, but they were clean, furnished, and central. In short, they were exactly what she and Naomi were looking for.

The bell above the shop door jangled. Sharon straightened, ready to serve the first customer of the day. Her jaw muscles slackened at the sight of the man striding into the shop, police hat off-center, drawing attention to his adorably lopsided ears.

Brian's mouth opened and shut a couple of times before words came out. "Morning, ladies."

"I have your order ready."

Sharon spun round at the sound of her boss's voice. Bridie didn't meet her eye.

"Ah, yeah." The flush on Brian's cheeks deepened. For some bizarre reason, his tendency to blush charmed her. The rosy tinge added color to his freckled cheeks, complementing his auburn hair. She'd bet he'd been teased at school for that hair. Yet it was a gorgeous shade of rich red—browner in winter and redder in summer. Not for the first time, she resisted the urge to run her fingers through it, muss it up good and proper. Wouldn't he freak out if she tried!

Brian approached Bridie and the cash register, but his wary gaze was trained on Sharon.

Her boss reached under the counter and withdrew a plastic bag. Sharon itched to know what it contained. Books, yeah, but which ones? She hadn't pegged Brian Glenn for a big reader.

"That'll be the amount we discussed," Bridie said, further fueling Sharon's curiosity. If she didn't know better, she'd have thought her boss was engaging in money laundering.

Brian slid his credit card into the card machine and typed in the code.

She didn't bother to feign disinterest. "Tell me, Garda Glenn, is Bridie catering to your secret penchant for *Fifty Shades of Grey?*"

"Sharon," Bridie said in a warning tone. "Garda Glenn is a customer. He placed an order, and I fulfilled it. It's not your place to speculate on his reading material."

Sharon folded her arms across her chest. "Oh, yeah? Because I'm imagining all sorts of naughty scenarios occurring in his *reading material.*"

Brian's pale blue gaze speared her in place, making her breath catch. "Don't judge me by your own low standards, Ms. MacCarthy. I might have fallen for your teasing over your bath product enterprise, but I'm not enough of an eejit to buy erotic literature from my local book shop."

She leaned forward, watching his gaze fasten on her cleavage before darting away. He really did blush beautifully, right to the tips of his ears. "In that case, online vendors are your friends."

Bridie shoved a book bag across the counter. "Here you go, Brian."

"Thanks, Bridie. Have a good day."

"You too. And good luck."

As he headed for the door, he gave Sharon a reluctant half smile. "Thanks for the eggs. They made a fine fry-up."

She shot him a wicked grin. "I'm delighted to have... satisfied your appetites, Garda Glenn. Enjoy the books."

His smile evaporated in an instant. "I'm sure I will," he said stiffly. "A good day to you."

"Ah, Sharon," Bridie said after the door had closed behind him. "You'll never get him to ask you out if you keep tormenting him."

She squawked in protest. "Why would you think I'd want to go out with that eejit?"

"The constant teasing is a dead giveaway. Have a care, will you? Brian can cope with a bit of slagging, but I think you hurt his feelings."

"How? I was only messing."

"Sometimes you take the joking too far."

Had she really hurt his feelings? *Damn.* She hadn't meant to offend him. "I don't know why you think I want Brian Glenn to ask me out. He's not my type, and I'm certain I'm not his."

At least the latter part of that spiel is true. Sharon's chest tightened, and her determined good cheer deflated quicker than a burst balloon. She wasn't sure why she was attracted to Brian Glenn. Perhaps it was his earnest, dependable nature—or maybe it was because he was as unlike her father as it was possible to get. "Last I heard, he was dating a policewoman from Cork City. He'd hardly choose the likes of me over someone with a sensible job." *And, presumably, a sensible family.*

"Don't be so hard on yourself. You've a lot to offer. Your problem is that you sell yourself short and end up with men who don't treat you with the respect you deserve."

A collage of past boyfriends danced through her mind. "Respect" wasn't a word she'd associate with any of them. To be fair, she'd taken them as seriously as they had her—which was to say not at all.

Giving herself a mental shake, she thrust back her shoulders and crossed her arms under her breasts. "Forget Brian Glenn. I'll have no time for romance until I get my degree. I'll be too busy studying to think about men."

"Indeed?" Bridie gave a sly smirk. "Are there no interesting fellas at university?"

"None that interest me."

"What about in your lectures and seminars?"

She shrugged. "I won't know until I attend forensic psychology this evening. I doubt it, though. The psych guys tend to be total nerds."

Bridie's shoulders were heaving.

Sharon blinked in confusion. "What's so funny?"

"Never you mind," her boss said between bouts of laughter. "I'm sure your semester will get off to a studious start."

36

CHAPTER FOUR

....

The lecture hall was housed in a modern circular building with dramatic floor-to-ceiling windows and tiered rows of plastic seats, fold-up writing desks attached to their sides. On the podium, a frizzy-haired professor was battling with an army of cables, none of which appeared to fit his portable computer.

Brian weaved his way through the rows, opting for an aisle seat in the middle of the room, neither too near the exit at the back nor too close to the stage at the front. The choice was made on autopilot—apparently, old habits were hard to break. Back when he was at secondary school, he'd always taken an aisle seat in the middle of the classroom. Sit too close to the teacher, and you were deemed a brown-noser; sit too close to the back, and you were labeled a potential troublemaker. As in most areas of his life, Brian preferred not to stand out.

He pulled his laptop out of his bag and placed it on the fold-up desk now stretched across his legs. Typing lecture notes made a pleasant change from scribbling witness statements, that was for sure. He peered around the packed lecture hall. Who knew forensic psychology was such a popular subject?

After three years of taking distance courses, he was officially enrolled as a part-time student at University

College Cork. He fairly glowed with pride. He'd never paid much attention to his schoolwork when he was a kid, doing well enough to pass all his exams and meet the grades required to join the police force but not excelling at any particular subject. Once he'd completed the initial three years of grunt work on the force, he'd realized he was qualified to do little else and was unlikely to rise beyond the basic rank of *garda*. So he'd applied for an Open University course and worked his arse off, squeezing in time to study around long hours on the job. To his surprise, he'd done well. At Seán's urging, he'd applied to University College Cork to complete his degree and was now enrolled as a part-time student. Two weeks into the semester, he was enjoying every second of his studies.

He shifted in his seat and fingered his collar absently. The casual jeans and shirt made him feel strange. He was so used to wearing his police uniform that he felt naked in civvies.

On the podium, the professor had found the correct cable. The first presentation slides flashed onto the screen. While the professor was clearing his throat to commence his lecture, the door to the hall creaked open. Brian glanced up from his laptop. And his jaw dropped.

In strutted a familiar form clad in a low-cut canary-yellow top and tight leather miniskirt. Her progress in her high heels could be described as tottering at best. Their eyes met, hers widening a fraction before her face split into a foxy grin. To his horror, she made a beeline for him. Batting improbably long mascaraed eyelashes, she plonked herself onto the empty seat next to his. "Hello, Garda Glenn. Fancy seeing you here."

"What the f—" He swallowed hard. "What are *you* doing here?"

Sharon's grin stretched wider, flashing pearly white teeth. "Same as you, I'd imagine. I need more credits to complete my psychology degree. This course was on my list of electives. What degree are you going for?"

"Criminology," he muttered.

"Ah," she said, smiling. "Apt, given your job. How come you're taking this course? I thought it was reserved for final-year students."

"I *am* a final-year student. I've spent the past couple of years taking OU courses."

"So that's why you were ordering mysterious books from Bridie."

"Yeah. She gives me a better discount than the campus bookshop."

"I'll bet she does." Sharon's voice was laced with laughter. "Is this is your first on-campus course?"

"Yeah."

"Must be quite a change. I almost didn't recognize you out of uniform." She tugged at his shirt playfully, sending a jolt of lust zigzagging to his groin.

He removed her hand from his chest and placed it firmly on her fold-up desk, ignoring the mischievous twinkle in her eye. "You're late starting this course. Did you switch classes?"

Her smile faltered. "No. I had... stuff to sort out after my mother died. Today is my first day back at uni." A look of raw emotion flitted across her face before the shutters slammed shut and the trademark cheeky grin was back in place.

"If you want to read over my lecture notes, I can e-mail them to you."

She leaned close, and her warm breath tickled his neck. "Are you looking for an excuse to get my e-mail address? Naughty, Garda Glenn."

"Settle down, everyone," boomed the professor before beginning his lecture.

For the first fifteen minutes, Brian was hyperaware of Sharon's presence in the seat beside him. Her sweet perfume teased his nose, and electric awareness skittered over his skin every time her arm brushed against his when she reached down for her bag. He exhaled sharply and tried to focus on the lecture. Thankfully, the professor was a compelling speaker and the material was interesting. The rest of the hour flew by.

He was finishing typing his notes when he felt Sharon's thigh press against him, jerking him out of the academic world of forensic psychology and back to the uncomfortable—not to mention hardening—awareness that he fancied Sharon MacCarthy.

"Not bad, eh?" She gathered up her stuff and shoved it into her shoulder bag. "Dr. Leech is less boring than most of the old geezers around here."

As if on cue, Dr. Leech's bombastic voice boomed through the microphone. "Just a minute, if you please. We're not finished yet. The semester project is to be completed in pairs. If you look at the following slide, you'll see I've matched each of you with another course participant. Wherever possible, I've paired people with different majors. I've also tried to take into account where you live so that you can more easily meet to study. Please consult your class list for your partner's contact info and get in touch with them between now and next week's lecture."

With a sense of foreboding prickling up his neck, Brian scanned the list until he found his name. *Oh, hell on wheels. No, no, no!*

Sharon hooted with laughter. "Well, would you look at that? We're research partners." She leaned in close, wafting perfume and sex appeal in equal measure. "Looks like you're stuck with me until December."

***

Sharon slung her book bag over her shoulder, shoved her phone between her teeth, and balanced a cardboard takeout tray containing two hot beverages. She backed against the study center's door, pushed it open, and maneuvered herself inside.

The study center was a new and welcome addition to the campus. Linked to the library via a small tunnel, it was designed to provide students with a comfortable space in which they could discuss their group projects without disturbing people studying in the library proper.

At a small table by a window, Brian was already hard at work on his laptop. A look of intense concentration creased his forehead, and his pen was poised to take notes. Her heart skipped a beat. He looked adorable and utterly kissable. Sharon smiled to herself. Her vow to avoid men this academic year had fallen to the wayside the second she'd clapped eyes on Brian across the crowded lecture hall. She'd had a crush on him for years, but he'd never regarded her as anything more than a criminal and a nuisance. This was her chance to prove him wrong.

"Well, hello there, Garda Glenn," she said in what she hoped was a sultry tone.

He glanced up from the screen, startled. "Hey." Shoving his chair back, he relieved her of the cardboard tray.

"I thought we could do with a hot sugary drink to aid our studies."

"Ah, thanks." He was eyeing the Styrofoam cups with suspicion.

"The one on the left is yours." At his wary expression, she added, "They're not poisoned. I swear."

He took a cautious sip from his cup, then blinked in surprise. "You got me tea."

"Yeah. You don't like coffee, right?"

"Right." He smiled, the first heartfelt smile he'd ever directed at her. Sharon's heart beat a little faster, and her legs went wobbly. Served her right for wearing towering high heels. She dropped her bag to the floor and slid into the seat opposite Brian's.

"So...," she said, unpacking her stuff. "What did you think of the research topic ideas I e-mailed you with?"

"They're good, yeah, especially the one on internet stalking. But we're going to need to narrow our focus."

She took a sip of coffee. "Okay. What do you suggest?"

"Given that we need to examine the psychology behind the issue, I think we should either focus on stalkers who harass their victims in a virtual public space or in a private one." He talked with his hands, subtle gestures at first, more expansive as he warmed to his topic. "So a public-space harasser could be someone who targets their victim-slash-victims on a social-media site and makes their abusive messages visible for all to see. They might use multiple accounts for the purpose, simply setting up new ones when the site blocks them for abuse."

"Right. In that case, a private-space harasser—insofar as anything on the internet is 'private'"—Sharon made quotation marks with her fingers—"is someone who targets their victims via e-mail or private message?"

"Exactly." His nod of approval made her glow from the inside out. "You're the psychology major. I'm guessing that a harasser's motivation would differ depending on how and where he or she perpetrates the abuse."

"You have a point, but it's more subtle than that. Someone who harasses another person openly via social media seeks to humiliate and embarrass them. Those who confine the abuse to e-mail and private messaging want to intimidate and frighten them. And even these are sweeping generalizations, because the motivations can spill over into one method or the other." She leaned forward, and they knocked knees. Maintaining a poker face, he shifted position and angled his chair, thus ensuring that they wouldn't bump up against one another again. So much for her powers of seduction.

"Why don't we focus on stalking via social media sites?" he said, moving his index finger over the trackpad. "I've a trove of info on Facebook, for example, because we've had to deal with a few instances of it at the station."

"Sounds good. We'll have to read some of the general texts and articles from our required reading list. Why don't we divide them up and compare notes?"

"Between now and next week, I'll compile a list of legal source material and police records we can use for the project. We'll need permission to use some of it, but I can sort that out. Emma—my ex—works for the internet crime division. I might be able to swing an interview or two with the people in her department."

His ex... the butterflies in Sharon's stomach took flight. Perhaps there was hope for her after all. She pulled her chair closer to Brian's laptop on the pretense of getting a closer look at the notes he was typing. This time, he didn't move away when her thigh pressed against his. She registered his sudden intake of breath and the flicker of awareness in his eyes.

"If you take care of the criminal side of the research, I'll focus on the psychological aspect. I attended a lecture by a forensic psychologist last semester on revenge porn. I'll e-mail her to see if she'd be willing to have a chat with me."

To her amusement, Brian was scribbling notes with one hand while typing with the other.

"How do you manage that?"

"Huh?" He considered her for a second. "Oh, the writing-typing combo. Practice. I have to do a lot of paperwork as part of my job. Actually, I spend more hours on admin than I do out of the station. If I get promoted, I'll have even more of it to do."

She leaned her elbows on the table and stared into his light blue eyes. They reminded her of the sky on a warm summer day. "Are you doing a degree to help you get ahead in the police force?"

"Yeah. At least, that was my motivation for starting one. If I don't get some sort of qualification, I'll keep treading water and stay at the rank of *garda* until I retire." He spun his pen between two fingers in a windmill fashion. He had nice hands. Big, strong, dependable. Sort of like the man himself.

"How are you finding the academic side of it?"

"Challenging, but I'm surprised at how much I'm enjoying it." He set the pen down and drained the last of his tea before tossing the cup into the wastepaper basket beside their table. "What about you? Do you like psychology?"

"Yeah, I do. I started out studying sociology but switched to psychology after my first semester. I'll admit I haven't always been a model student, but I've done well enough to scrape a pass in my exams. This year, though, it'll be different."

"Because your mother died." It was a statement, not a question.

"Yeah. I told her I'd knuckle down and finish my degree. I need to think of my future. I don't fancy staying on the farm and being treated like crap by my dad for the rest of my life, so I need to get a job that pays more than the minimum wage. Only way to do that these days is to have a degree. Even then..." She shrugged.

"Most employers will tell you to get a postgrad degree," he finished for her.

"Exactly. At least with psychology, I can get part-time work at a clinic or children's home while I'm getting my master's."

"Sounds like you've got it all worked out." He smiled again—a warm, wide grin that melted her insides and turned her mind to mush.

"It's all dependent on me getting good grades this year." Not to mention escaping the farm and her father. If she didn't get away from the caustic atmosphere, she'd fall apart before Christmas.

"In that case, let's make sure this research paper rocks." Brian closed his laptop and slid it into its protective case. "Can I give you a lift back to Ballybeg? I need to squeeze in a couple of hours at the station."

"Thanks, but I have to hit the library."

"Sensible girl." He stood, then hovered awkwardly, the self-possession of earlier ebbing away with each second. "I'm glad you're my partner," he said finally, a serious expression on his face. "I think we'll work well together over the next few months."

"I'm delighted to be your new partner." She let the innuendo linger in the air, noted the familiar blush stain his cheeks once he registered the double entendre. If she played her cards right, they'd be doing a lot more than working together. In her opinion, Garda Brian Glenn was in desperate need of a girlfriend who'd ignite his wild side. She fully intended to be that woman.

CHAPTER FIVE

....

Within a couple of weeks of being partnered with Sharon for the semester project, Brian had fallen into the surprisingly comfortable pattern of studying with her twice a week. Sometimes, they'd go out to a café or a pub after they'd finished their work. Other times, they'd part on the steps of the study center.

Regardless of where they took their leave of one another, there was always an odd, electrically charged tug-of-war between them. The urge to kiss her was overwhelming. He'd always had a crush on Sharon MacCarthy, even if he'd been loath to admit it to himself.

Outside Ballybeg, she was a toned-down version of the brash, insouciant charmer who'd both fascinated and infuriated him in the four years he'd lived there. Her crazy dress sense was the same, regardless of the setting, but her humor was wittier, and her sharp intelligence was a pleasant surprise. By constantly telling him, herself, and—presumably—the world, that she'd never be as smart as her older brother, Sharon was selling herself short.

"So," he said, shutting his laptop, "want to relocate to a nonacademic environment?"

Her throaty laugh was infectious. "I could murder a burger."

"Now, now. Careful what you say in front of a cop."
He returned her grin and sensed the heat between them
as keenly as if it were an erotic caress. "How about the
new place on Penrose Quay? My treat. They're supposed
to serve great gourmet burgers and American-style
fries."

"My mouth is watering at the very thought." She
grabbed her book bag and followed him out into the
crisp October evening. They took the bus into the city
center. The Christmas lights would soon be out, and he
couldn't wait. Brian loved Christmas. The lead up to it,
the day itself, and the aftermath. He also loved Cork
City, which surprised him. He'd grown up on a farm in
Donegal. His first exposure to a city was a day excursion
to Belfast when he was eight. He'd hated the experience.
The crowds were claustrophobic, the shops too large, the
hustle and bustle too fast. Whether it was being an adult
or a preference for the lazier pace, he liked Cork City,
and the upstairs front row on the double-decker bus
afforded him an excellent view of the River Lee.

Sharon's heel caught on the step as they alighted
from the bus, sending her stumbling into him.

He held her steady. "You okay?"

"I'm fine. I'm not wearing bus-friendly footwear."

He grinned down at her sparkly blue stiletto heels. "I
wouldn't say those shoes are safe in any circumstances."

"What can I say? I like fancy shoes, even if they don't
always like me."

49

"Come on." He linked arms with her, noting her surprise that was quickly followed by a teasing grin. He propelled her into motion. "Let's find our restaurant. I'm starving."

They found Tommy's Bar and Grill with ease. Despite it being packed, they didn't have to wait longer than fifteen minutes to get a table.

Sharon peered at him over the enormous menu. She'd opted for pink sparkly eye shadow today and navy eyelashes. It should have looked garish. And, in a way, it did. If any woman could pull off garish, it was Sharon. "What are you having?" she asked.

"I'm debating between the double hamburger with avocado and bacon, or its Swiss cheese and relish equivalent."

She perused the menu. "I'm going for the blue cheese burger with a side order of crinkly fries."

"Sounds delicious. Are you having a drink? Might as well, seeing as we're both taking public transport back to Ballybeg."

Her plump lips curved into a smile. "A glass of Merlot would go down nicely."

"In that case, I'll order a bottle."

"Ooh," she teased, "sounds like we're making a night of it."

"I guess we are," he said, suddenly serious.

Their eyes met for an elongated moment. To his amazement, Sharon's face grew pink. He reached out and stroked her cheek. The skin under his fingertips was silky soft. "Isn't turning red as a fire engine supposed to be my role?"

"I'm not blushing." She fanned herself wildly. "It's the heat in here."

"Yeah, right." His fingers skimmed her chin. The sensation sent a jolt of longing vibrating through his body. From the way her eyes widened, then clouded with lust, he was having a similar effect on her. He leaned closer, his mouth hovering a few centimeters from hers.

At that moment, the waiter materialized to take their order. Exhaling a whistle, Brian released Sharon's chin and drew back. Within a couple of minutes, the waiter had furnished them with wine glasses and a carafe of rich red liquid.

"*Sláinte.*" Brian clinked his glass against Sharon's. When his fingers touched hers, her sharp intake of breath acted like a fan to his already inflamed libido. "I owe you an apology."

She blinked in surprise. "For what?"

"For jumping to conclusions about you. The Book Mark vandalism, the bath bombs... I'm sorry."

"To be fair, I gave you plenty of reasons to suspect me of all sorts during your first couple of years in Ballybeg. I'm no saint."

He laughed. "No, you're definitely not, but as far as I'm aware, you haven't done anything illegal for over two years."

"Nothing you've caught me for." Sharon grinned over the rim of her wine glass, then grew serious. "I don't want to end up like my father and brothers. Apart from Ruairí, they've all done time. And I definitely don't want to end up like my mother—married to a loser with a passel of kids and no money. A degree won't guarantee I'll have a better life than she did, but it's a step in the right direction."

"Yes, it is." He reached across the table and took her hands. "All the more reason to make sure our semester project is the best we can make it."

"Why are you doing a degree? Do you need one for work?"

He nodded. "If I want a promotion, I need something to make me stand out. It's not like I'll get it through solving complicated crimes in Ballybeg."

"Do you want to become a detective or something? No offense, but you've never struck me as wildly ambitious."

"No offense taken. I'm not ambitious in the way Seán Mackey is. I don't need a fancy office and a personal driver, and I actually like policing a small area like Ballybeg. I did my training in Dublin and hated it. Couldn't wait to escape. I was delighted to be posted down here. I grew up in a village, and that's the sort of community I want to live in."

"So why the driving need to get a degree?"

"I don't want to stay at the rank of *garda* for the rest of my career. Some day"—he felt himself blush to the roots of his red hair—"I'd like to settle down and have a family. Hard to raise kids on my current salary. A higher rank means better money." It would also mean more esteem at the station. He was growing tired of the older reserve policemen taking the piss out of him even though he was a full-timer and outranked them.

The waiter arrived with their order, and the meal passed in a haze of sensory impressions. The food more than lived up to the restaurant's reputation. Every bite brought him closer to Sharon. Their hands brushed repeatedly, and he nearly shot out of his chair when she put a tentative hand on his thigh followed by a foot trailing up his calf. At some point during the meal, she must have slipped off those sexy blue sparkly shoes. He'd never seen her bare feet. Tonight, he intended to remedy that situation. "You sure you're ready for this? It's not too soon after your mother..."

"Oh, come on." She rolled her eyes and laughed. "It's inevitable. We've been leading one another on a merry dance these past few weeks. I'm starting to get dizzy."

He squeezed her hands. "I don't want to take advantage of you while you're feeling vulnerable."

Sharon threw her head back and roared with laughter. "Vulnerable? Me? I'm tough as nails."

"You like to think you are at any rate. I don't want you to—"

"Don't." She held up a palm. The smile was still in place but her lips seemed frozen. "There's a laundry list of reasons why we wouldn't work, but who says we need to get serious? I'm too busy for a relationship. I'm guessing you are too."

"That not what I—" He broke off, sensing the unease form a barrier between them. Bringing up her mother's death had been a mistake, but deleting the last few sentences wasn't an option. What he'd intended to say was that he wasn't a casual fling kind of guy, but if sex was all she wanted from him, he'd roll with the situation. He took her hand in his and stroked her inside wrist, feeling her pulse skitter under his fingertips. "We both know this is going to happen. I'm making a last-ditch attempt at being sensible."

Her foot scooted further up his thigh. "Being sensible is overrated."

His gaze skimmed her plump lips, smooth white neck, and creamy cleavage, then refocused on her warm brown eyes. "Okay, let's take it one step at a time. Do you want to come back to my place?"

Her lips parted in a squeal. "And get to see the Batcave? Definitely!"

"Batcave?" he laughed. "You know where I live. Everyone in Ballybeg does. It's no secret."

"True. But I've imagined all sorts of things about your house. You're so sensible and correct. A secret sex dungeon is practically a given, complete with implements of torture."

"As I have no basement, you're in for a disappointment. I do have an impressive liquor cabinet, though. I worked part-time in a cocktail bar while I was at police college."

"Can you make cocktails?"

She'd lowered her voice to a husky whisper, sending his heart rate into acceleration mode.

"I certainly can."

Sharon leaned closer and rubbed her nose against his, Eskimo-style. "Batcave, cocktails, and potentially mind-blowing sex? Let's go!"

CHAPTER SIX

··

The Batcave proved to be a small two-up-two-down terrace house in the less-than-salubrious part of Ballybeg.

"You live near my Uncle Buck," Sharon said cheerfully. "Not to mention his pal John-Joe Fitzgerald. That must be fun for you."

Brian paused in the act of inserting his key in the door. "Oh, yeah. They're fantastic neighbors. I'm constantly having to avert my eyes in case I see them up to something illegal on my day off. That pair of eejits is involved in every dodgy get-rich-quick scheme in Ballybeg."

He opened the door and gestured for her to enter. Sharon took off her coat and scarf and surveyed her surroundings. The entrance hall was narrow and led to a small galley kitchen at the back of the house. A door to the right opened to reveal a tiny living room crammed with an overlarge sofa and two armchairs so stuffed they looked like they were on steroids.

Brian closed the curtains and made a beeline for a large drinks cabinet next to a wide, flat-screen television. "What are you having? I don't have much in the way of fruit, but there are a few limes and oranges in the kitchen."

"Can you make me a vodka gimlet?"

He smiled, and when he did so, the corners of his eyes creased adorably, making her heart skip a beat. "I certainly can." A few minutes later, he pressed a cocktail glass into her hand. "Enjoy."

"Thanks. This looks delicious." It tasted delicious too. She watched him mix his own cocktail. He'd opted for a whiskey sour with a slice of orange to decorate.

"So," he said, raising his glass. "To our research project. May we come top of the class."

"I'll drink to that. I'm an eternal optimist."

Their glasses clinked, making a pleasant ringing noise. Instead of stepping apart, Brian closed the space between them and planted a soft kiss on her nose. Her breath caught as he trailed kisses lower before claiming her mouth with his. He tasted divine—whiskey mingled with peppermint gum. She pulled him closer, hungry for more, relishing the musky scent of his aftershave and the sensation of his thick red hair running through her fingers.

The room spun around her, and she belatedly remembered she still had her eyes open, gawping like a teenager. She'd known he'd kiss her when he'd invited her back to his place, and she'd expected to like it. But she hadn't anticipated a reaction this strong. She pressed her breasts against his chest and felt his heart beating, skimmed her hands down his shirt, noting the hard muscles beneath. He groaned and deepened the kiss.

"We'd better get rid of these glasses," she murmured into his neck.

He whisked hers out of her hand and put both glasses on the coffee table. Pushing her back on the sofa, Brian applied himself to the task of making her swoon. He proved most adept at the job. She gasped when he trailed kisses down her neck and over her cleavage.

"You have gorgeous breasts," he murmured, voice thick with desire. "I've imagined what they'd feel like for so long."

"Is that so?" she teased, tracing the freckles on his nose. "If you've been imagining them, maybe you'd like to see them." She sat up and pulled her top over her head, revealing her favorite red and black lacy bra. He sucked in a breath, and his pupils dilated. The sight of his obvious desire was a major turn-on. "Do you like what you see?" She toyed with the straps. "Do you want to see more?"

"Yeah," he croaked. "Definitely."

She unhooked the strap at the back and eased the bra over her breasts.

"Whoa. They're beautiful. *You're* beautiful."

She laughed. "I'm not, and you know it. But if I do say so myself, I lucked out in the boob department."

He cupped her chin in his palms. "You're beautiful to me."

He said the words with such conviction that she believed him. She blinked back unexpected tears. Had anyone called her beautiful before? Doubtful. "Who knew you were such a charmer, Garda Glenn?" she said, determined to diffuse the warm tenderness that was threatening to unravel the barbed wire guarding her heart.

Taking his hand, she guided him over her breasts, remaining in charge at first but soon giving way to his need to explore. The sensation of his hands on her skin was electric. He teased one of her nipples, making her moan, then trailed his other hand down her stomach. For once, she was too preoccupied with the sensations rolling over her to feel self-conscious over her fleshy abdomen. She wasn't fat, but she definitely wasn't thin, and her natural build didn't lend itself to washboard abs. Brian didn't seem to care.

"Gorgeous," he murmured, kissing her belly and pulsing his tongue around her navel.

Breath caught in her throat. She tugged impatiently at his shirt and began to unbutton it. She'd gotten halfway down his chest when he pulled the garment over his head and tossed it onto the floor. Now it was her turn to ogle him. As she'd suspected, he had well-defined muscles. A smattering of hair decorated his upper chest, but his torso was otherwise smooth and solid. She ran her palms all the way down his front and tugged at his belt. "Off."

He leaned forward to nibble her ear. "Ladies first."

That made her laugh. "I've been accused of many things in my time. Being a lady is not one of them. But I'll play along."

She eased her jeans over her hips and down her legs. While she was removing her socks, he was already removing her lacy knickers. "Very sexy," he said, holding his prize aloft.

"If you're so fond of them, I'll buy you a pair."

"Somehow I don't think they'd look as good on me as they do off you," he said with a rueful smile.

She indicated his crotch, the telltale bulge in his underwear making her wet and achy with longing. "Now it's your turn."

He slid off his underwear, revealing the hard smoothness of his erection.

"Whoa." Her hand reached out as if by its own volition. She stroked the silky skin of his shaft and heard his ragged breathing when she bent down to tease the tip with her tongue.

"Careful," he groaned. "It's been a while. I don't want to come too soon."

He pushed her back on the sofa and teased the sensitive skin on her inside thighs. When his tongue found her clit, she arched her back and gasped. Most men, in her not insubstantial experience, wouldn't be able to find their way around the female genitalia with the aid of GPS. Clearly Brian was not "most men." He teased her with circular movements, dancing his tongue forward and back. The friction combined with the sensation of his stubble tickling her thighs made her cry out with pleasure.

"That feels so good," she whispered, stroking his hair. "I don't suppose your handcuffs are nearby?"

"Handcuffs?" His head came up, and he spluttered with laughter. "Isn't this the point where you ask me if I have a condom?"

"Knowing your personality, I'd be shocked if you *didn't* have one." She arched forward. "Now about those handcuffs..."

"All right. Wait a sec." He staggered to his feet and went into the hall. A minute later, he returned, armed with his police handcuffs and a small key. "I'm not supposed to use these for—"

"Sex play?" She pushed herself up on her elbows and watched his gaze fasten on her naked breasts.

"Yeah."

"And how many of your colleagues disobey that order, I wonder?"

His smile widened. "Probably all."

"Throw them here." She caught the handcuffs, then weighed the cold metal in her hands. "They're heavier than I expected."

"That's because they're real handcuffs, not the fakes you buy in sex shops."

"I'm sure we could decorate these with fluffy pink material."

"I'll pass, thanks," he said dryly. "I don't fancy clapping pink fluffy handcuffs on the likes of John-Joe Fitzgerald the next time I arrest him."

"Come here," she murmured, reaching for him. He obeyed, kissing her, stroking her breasts, belly, thighs, and between her legs, driving her to distraction. "I want you inside me."

In one fluid movement, he caught her wrists above her head and handcuffed her.

The hard restraints chafed against her skin, but the feeling was a turn-on, especially with Brian watching her with a wicked gleam in his eyes. "You won't be going anywhere fast, Ms. MacCarthy."

"Hey," she protested, laughing. "I was going to handcuff *you*."

"I know. You can save that for Round Two." He flashed her a smile tinged with naughtiness and raw sexual desire. Then he ripped open a condom foil and rolled it over his shaft. "For the moment," he murmured against her neck, "you're my prisoner."

"Well, you were always trying to lock me up, weren't you?" She gasped when she felt the tip of his shaft tease her entrance. "Looks. Like. You. Succeeded."

"Looks. Like." The soft aroma of his shampoo teased her senses as he buried his head into her neck.

She helped him find her entrance, arranging the position of her hips to accommodate him. He was bigger than she'd expected. The first thrust was a shock, but her body soon adjusted to his size.

"You're fabulous," he whispered into her ear as he moved inside her. "Absolutely perfect."

She looped her handcuffed arms around his neck and tried to answer, but the only sound she emitted was a moan of pleasure. The pressure in her groin built with each thrust, further enhanced by his hand tugging on her nipple.

She pulled him closer, moving her hips to allow him deeper penetration. Lost to sensation, she let the feelings build until they came in a simultaneous explosion of ecstasy. When she cried out, he swallowed her scream with a kiss.

Afterward they lay on the sofa, panting. He took her hand and squeezed it. "That was even better than my most X-rated fantasies. You are an amazing woman, Sharon MacCarthy."

"I'm also a *restrained* woman." She jangled the handcuffs.

"Oh, yeah," he said with a laugh. "I'd forgotten about those."

Leaping off the sofa, he grabbed the key from the coffee table. He gently held her wrists as he unlocked her. This was the moment she'd been waiting for. As soon as the handcuffs slackened around her wrists, she removed them and clamped one of them around Brian's left hand, lightning fast, and the other to the radiator beside the sofa. "Hey," he protested. "Careful of the key." A clinking sound of metal falling against metal rang from behind the radiator. Sharon's eyes flew to his, and saw her frozen shock reflected. "Oh, feck."

CHAPTER SEVEN

....

B rian regarded his wrist with horror, then turned his attention to Sharon. She was naked, beautiful, and sexy as hell. And if he weren't facing the prospect of ending his days chained to his living room radiator, he'd want to make love to her all over again. "The key was in the lock. Please don't tell me it fell behind the radiator."

"Maybe it hit the floor." She got to her knees and scrambled round the carpet, affording him an excellent view of her shapely arse.

"No luck?"

"No," she moaned and shoved a lock of wild hair out of her face. The sparkly eye shadow he'd admired earlier was now gloriously smudged. She looked fucked and fuckable. He was getting hard just looking at her.

"Did you hear that clang of metal when I handcuffed you?" she asked. "Like something falling behind the radiator?"

"I did, but I really didn't want to believe it. If the key's behind there"—he jerked his thumb at the wall-mounted radiator—"we'll have a hell of a time getting it back out."

"Oh, no," she said in a tone of despair, then caught his eye and dissolved into a fit of maniacal laughter. "What are we going to do?"

"I'm at the wrong angle to check behind the radiator. You'll have to do it. There's a flashlight on the mantelpiece."

Sharon leaped up and got the flashlight. She shone its thin beam of light behind the radiator. And swore.

"Can you see it?"

"No. It's got to be there, though. How else are we going to get you free?"

"I don't suppose one of your family members taught you how to pick a lock?"

"Alas, no. We MacCarthys aren't that subtle. We're more the smash-the-window or break-the-door-down types." She tried to reach down the back of the radiator, but her hand wouldn't fit. "Ouch." She recoiled and clutched her hand. "That thing's hot. So how are we going to get you free?"

"By calling Seán Mackey," he said gloomily. "He can get the spare key for these cuffs from the station." At least Seán would be discreet and not tell the entire station about Brian's predicament. Teasing him when they were alone was another story.

"What's his number?" Sharon had already retrieved her sparkly smart phone from her handbag.

"My phone is in the back pocket of my jeans. It's saved under my contacts."

Twenty minutes later, Seán strode into the living room, wearing a shit-eating grin and more respectable attire than the towel Sharon had draped around Brian's waist. Sharon herself had gone on a mad clothes retrieval spree and was dressed—more or less.

Seán's gaze trailed over the post-coital chaos of the living room before settling on Brian's restrained wrist. "This has got to be the best emergency call out of my career."

Brian shifted uncomfortably on the sofa, angling his wrist away from the heat of the radiator. "Go on, have a good laugh. But could you please unlock me between bursts of hysteria?"

Seán rocked back on his heels, prolonging his partner's agony. "Well, well. So you two finally got it on."

"So we did," Sharon said, folding her arms across her chest and fixing the police sergeant with a fulminating glare. "Now are you going to unlock him so we can 'get it on' again?"

"Sharon!" Embarrassment burned a path to Brian's scalp. "Do you have to be so—"

She arched an eyebrow. "Direct? You knew what you were getting when you asked me out, Garda Glenn. Want to back out now?"

"Hell, no." He turned to his partner. "Hop with those keys, man."

"Gladly," Seán said in mock alarm. "I need to get out of here before I witness a porn scene." He flipped a key out of his pocket and slid it into the handcuff's narrow lock.

The cuff loosened around Brian's wrist. He wriggled free and stood, clutching the inadequately small towel around his waist. "Thanks, man. I owe you one."

Seán's grin slid back into place. "No thanks needed. This rescue mission was the highlight of my evening." He spun on his heel and headed for the living room door, then paused in the doorframe and saluted them. "Have fun, kids."

After the front door slammed behind Seán, they looked at one another. Sharon gave a sly half smile and pulled off her top to reveal... absolutely nothing... underneath. The sight of her naked breasts made him rock hard and wild with longing. "You're torturing me," he growled. "Come here."

She obeyed, standing demurely in front of him. Then her lips curved, and she sank to her knees. "Would you like me to spend the night with you, Garda Glenn?"

"I'd like you to spend *every* night with me if it means sex this hot."

Her deep laugh reverberated against his thigh. Then she put her mouth over his shaft, and then he ceased to think until morning.

***

Sharon adjusted her witch's hat and slid a pint across the counter to a thirsty customer. It was Halloween and her turn to help out in the family pub. Her brother Ruairí's pub to be precise, since he'd bought it from their parents a couple of years ago. He'd spent time and money restoring the place to its former glory. She appreciated his insistence that MacCarthy's retain its old-fashioned look combined with modern comforts. Tonight the pub was festooned with fake cobwebs, pumpkins, and skeletons. Most of the patrons had embraced the spirit of the holiday and donned costumes —some scary, some risqué, some utterly absurd.

"All right?" Ruairí reached underneath the counter for a fresh pint glass and sent his pirate hat askew in the process.

"I'm grand. Yourself?"

"Fine." A small smile played at the corners of his mouth. "More than fine."

She gave him a bear hug. "You'll make a great daddy, bro. Jayme's lucky to have you."

"I'm lucky to have her." He beamed and disentangled himself from her fake witchy talons. "This pregnancy seems to be dragging, though. Seems forever until March."

"I'll remind you of this conversation when you're haggard from lack of sleep. Will it be a St. Patrick's Day baby?"

"He or she is due on the nineteenth of March, so it's a possibility."

"Fingers crossed. We have no little Paddy in our family."

Her brother grimaced. "If Jayme has her way, we won't have one in March, either."

"What names does she like?" Sharon was fond of her American sister-in-law, but their disparate backgrounds caused the occasional difference of opinion or culture clash.

Her brother wrinkled his slightly crooked nose. "If the baby is a girl, Jayme wants to call her Lucrezia."

"As in Borgia?" Sharon roared with laughter. "Ah, no. I can't see that name flying in Ballybeg. You'll have to talk her down."

"I'm doing my best." Ruairí's smile turned sly. "Speaking of romance, I hear you're spending a lot of time with a certain policeman."

Sharon felt her cheeks turn pink. "Would you have a problem if I were?"

"Not at all. Just surprised. Glenn's not your usual type."

"No, he certainly isn't." *And thank goodness for that.* In the fortnight since they'd first slept together, Sharon had spent at least a couple of nights a week at Brian's house. It served a number of purposes—apart from the obvious benefit of the amazing sex. First, it got her off the farm and away from Da. Second, Brian had no problem with her staying on at his place to study when he headed out to work in the morning. And last but definitely not least, Brian himself. She'd never been short of men to date, but she'd gravitated toward the reckless bad-boy type and had never expected—or wanted—the relationships to last.

Until now.

And that was the part that scared the bejaysus out of her. Brian was different. He listened when she talked.

Really listened. He made her hot milky coffee when she had a crying jag about her mother. He let her rant about Da and never once said a word about the number of times he'd had to deal with the man in his role as cop. And he treated her with respect. None of her previous boyfriends had done that, and the difference in how it made her feel about him, about herself, and about their relationship was a revelation.

"I like Brian," she admitted. "I like him a lot."

The corners of Ruairí's warm brown eyes creased in concern. "I know you do, kiddo. And that's what worries me. I don't want to see you get hurt."

She placed her hands on her hips. "Well, aren't you the hypocrite. You were always complaining about my boyfriends. Now I find a fella with a steady job, and you're still bellyaching."

He held up his palms in surrender. "Calm down, sis. I had no time for those other eejits because they were likely to lead you into trouble. Brian Glenn is a decent bloke."

"So what's the problem?"

He patted her on the head just as he'd done when she was a little girl. "I don't want to see you with a broken heart."

She swallowed past the lump in her throat. "When he dumps me for someone more suitable, you mean?"

Her brother shook his head. "I was thinking more along the lines of when you screw it up and he ends the relationship."

His words burned like acid on her skin. She drew back, wounded. "Why does everyone in this town have such a low opinion of me?"

"They don't." Ruairí took her shoulders. "I don't."

"And I certainly don't," said a very familiar Donegal-accented voice.

Sharon jerked round to see Brian standing at the counter, looking both ridiculous and ridiculously sexy in a glam rock vampire costume. "It was all Nora Fitzgerald had left at her suit-rental shop," he said by way of explanation. "I left it a little late to book my costume."

Beside Brian stood her sister Marcella, resplendent in a leprechaun outfit, complete with a pot of gold around her already substantial waist. She'd even dyed the tips of her spiky peroxide hair green for the occasion. "Hey, Sharon. I promised lover boy here"—a jerk of a thumb in Brian's direction—"that I'd release you from your duties."

Brian gave an exaggerated shrug of his shoulders. "What can I say? We met in Nora's costume section. I persuaded Marcella to work your shift and let me spirit you into the night."

"In other words, he bribed me," Marcella said cheerily, maneuvering her wide costume behind the counter. "He's doubling my wage for the night. More moolah for my Christmas trip away with Máire. How could I refuse?"

"Well, well," Sharon teased. "I thought you were above resorting to bribery, Garda Glenn."

His gaze roved her naughty witch ensemble. "Cute outfit, but you're going to need a warm coat for where we're going."

"I'm intrigued." She grabbed her coat from a hook beneath the counter and turned to her brother. "See you, bro. Have fun rescuing glasses from Marcella's costume."

"Oy," her sister said. "Don't be so cheeky. It took a lot of time and effort to look this bad."

Ruairí winked at Sharon. "I'll safeguard the glasses. Have a nice evening."

"I intend to have a nice *night*." Sharon whacked Brian on the behind. "Right, Garda Glenn?"

His wicked grin sent a tingle down her spine. "Let's see how enthusiastic you are when you see *where* we're going."

....

CHAPTER EIGHT

Fifteen minutes later, Brian pulled into his designated parking space outside Ballybeg Garda Station. It was lashing rain outside, causing rivulets of water to cascade down the windshield. He cast an impish grin at his passenger. "What do you think of our secret destination?"

Sharon let out a hoot. "What's this? Are you arresting me again?"

"Nope. Impromptu Halloween party."

He climbed out of the car and held the passenger door open for her. "Mind the puddle. The car park is riddled with pot holes."

Inside the station, buckets had been placed at strategic intervals to catch water dripping from the numerous leaks in the roof. The two reserve policemen on duty had made a halfhearted attempt to decorate the lobby. Between the leaks and the damp in the walls, they didn't need to make much effort to turn the place into a house of horrors.

Sharon surveyed the mess. "This place is a total sinkhole. It's worse every time I'm here."

"I know. Thankfully, this is a good-bye-and-good-riddance party."

Her step faltered. "You're... leaving?"

"Yeah. Finally." He steered her in the direction of the station's tiny recreation room, past the leering stare of the older reserve *garda*. "I can't wait to get out of this dump."

"I see," her tone was subdued, her body language stiff, her heavily made-up face crumpled.

Wait, she doesn't think... "Sharon, no." They were outside his office, so he pulled her inside and shut the door. "I'm not leaving Ballybeg."

She stared at him through fake spidery eyelashes. "You're not?"

"Of course not. I wouldn't slip in something that important as a conversational aside."

Uncertainty clouded her eyes until she blinked it away and reverted to her customary bravado. "Then what did you mean?"

"The station is moving. The superintendent called us this afternoon to say the force is finally making good on the promise they made five years ago. This building will be razed and a new one constructed in its place. We'll be in prefabs for a while. Hardly ideal, but better than needing an umbrella in my office."

"Oh. Right." Her tinny laugh rang false.

How had they gone from joking and flirting one second to emotion-laden awkwardness the next? And how come loud and brassy Sharon MacCarthy was ten times less confident than his own bashful self?

He dropped a kiss on the tiny spider she'd painted on her nose. "Was it a mistake to bring you here? I did it on impulse. Thought it might give us both a laugh, considering all the times I've brought you to the station under different circumstances."

She emitted a small snort. "No, I get the joke. But when I assumed you were leaving Ballybeg... I guess I'm surprised by how much the idea upset me."

He cupped her chin in his hands. "Am I moving too fast for you? If so, I'm sorry. I haven't done casual in the past. I don't think I know how."

"You're not moving too fast, Brian. Truth be told, I've never been happier." Her tentative tone made his heart skip a beat. "Being able to *talk* to a man is weird, though. My Da... well, he's not exactly the warm fuzzy type. I love my brothers, but our relationship is based on teasing and fighting. Until I started going out with you, I saved all my emotional stuff for the women in my life."

He grinned down at her. "Let's just say the women in *my* life left me with no choice but to learn to express my emotions and listen to them express theirs. I grew up with three sisters, a mother, several aunts, and loads of girl cousins. Dad and I didn't stand a chance."

"How did they feel about you joining the police?"

"Not happy, but I needed to strike out on my own. I love them to bits, and I enjoy visiting, but they'd suffocate me if I lived there. My mother refuses to believe I can actually work a washing machine."

"Apart from Ruairí, my brothers genuinely *can't* work a washer. They expected Ma to do their laundry."

"And now they expect you to do it?"

She grimaced. "Spot on." She leaned in for a hug. "I'm glad you're not leaving Ballybeg."

He stroked her wild blond hair and bent down for another kiss. "The only place I want to be is where you are. Now what about a dance?"

She tugged on his hand. "Lead on."

The decorations in the recreation room were more lavish than those in the lobby. It was also the one room in the small police station building that sported *only* two leaks. Ballybeg Garda Station was relatively small and was responsible for the town of Ballybeg and several nearby villages. In addition to a superintendent who oversaw Ballybeg and two other stations, there were two full-time policemen (Brian and Seán), four reservists, and one part-time receptionist-cum-secretary. McGarry and Doyle were on duty tonight, and everyone else was swaying on the makeshift dance floor.

Brian and Sharon's entrance earned them a few stares: Some friendly, some wary, and—in O'Shaughnessy's case, some downright hostile. Brian put his arm around Sharon's waist. Screw anyone who objected to her being his date tonight.

Seán was manning the punch bowl. He ladled orange liquid into two plastic cups and shoved them across the counter. "Here you go."

Brian sniffed his cup. "Jaysus. What concoction is this?

"Pumpkin punch," Seán said. "Or so I've been informed. Tastes like vodka and orange juice with a few spices thrown in."

Sharon took a cautious sip. "Ugh. Vile."

Brian's own taste test brought him to the same conclusion.

"They should have waited for you to make cocktails," she said.

"Maybe." He dumped his cup beside her discarded one and coaxed her onto the dance floor. "But then I'd be on barman duty all evening, and I wouldn't get to dance with you."

A boppy chart-topper blasted through the speakers. Brian and Sharon twirled around with more enthusiasm than grace.

Three fast-paced tunes were followed by a slow song. They were enjoying a slow dance when Brian felt a blow between his shoulder blades.

"Well, would ye look what the cat dragged in." O'Shaughnessy leered at them through bloodshot eyes. If appearances were anything to go by, the retired police officer had liberally partaken of the pumpkin punch.

"Mind your manners." Brian heard the steely edge to his voice. "Sharon is my guest tonight, and I'll have her treated with respect."

O'Shaughnessy took another swig from his plastic cup, spilling most of the drink down his creased shirt. He jabbed a fat finger into Brian's chest. "I spent my career arresting her father. The whole family is bent.

You watch yourself, Glenn. Once she's had her laugh dating a policeman, she'll dump you for one of the lowlifes she usually lies down with."

Sharon was mad enough to emit sparks. "Piss off. I remember you barging into our house and beating the shite out of my father before cautioning him. Da is no saint, but neither are you."

O'Shaughnessy leaned close enough for them to smell the stale cigarettes on his breath. "You're nothing but a little tart. I don't care what sort of fancy course you're doing at university. You'll end up in the ditch like the rest of your family."

Having had prior experience with Sharon's temper when confronted with a belligerent police officer, Brian picked her up and swung her out of the line of fire. O'Shaughnessy, drunk though he was, had survival instinct. The old man lumbered to the side, clutching his crotch protectively.

"That prick," she snarled, struggling wildly to get free. "He deserves a good kick to the bollocks."

"Sharon," Brian cautioned, not letting her go. "We're in a police station, and he's a former police officer. However justified you feel in physically attacking him, it's not going to happen. Not on my watch."

"She's out of control," the older man muttered. "I'm only saying what everyone else thinks."

"No," Brian snapped, "you're saying what *you* think. Yeah, she has a temper, but you're behaving like a boor."

"Well, now," O'Shaughnessy sneered, "Fancy that. The young pup is developing claws."

"Go home, man. You're drunk and obnoxious."

Seán appeared at O'Shaughnessy's side. "Come on, you old eejit. Let's get you home. Brian's right. You've had a few too many."

The old man gripped Seán's hand as though it were a lifeline. "Ah, you were always a good lad, Johnny. I remember the time you—"

Seán's face registered alarm. "Right," he said with forced jollity, "I'll get this fella home. Have fun, kids. Don't do anything I wouldn't do."

Brian and Sharon gawped after the police sergeant hauling the by-now-limpid older officer out of the building.

"Johnny?" Sharon drew the name out, overemphasizing each syllable. "Seán's name is Johnny?"

"News to me." Brian squinted into the distance, thoughts tumbling through his mind. "I'm wondering how he knows O'Shaughnessy. Usually, the old fella rolls in for the Christmas party. Seán didn't start working here until February of this year."

"Hunh." Sharon gave a facial shrug. "Well, never mind about them. Why don't you and I skedaddle? The punch is crap, and I'm in the mood for one of your killer cocktails. Plus," she ran a hand down the satin shirt of his glam rock vampire costume, "I want to see what your fangs can do."

He dropped a dramatic kiss on her wrist, relishing the feel of her pulse quickening under his lips. "Your wish is my command."

CHAPTER NINE

....

The next few weeks passed in a blur. Between work, university, and Brian, Sharon succeeded in avoiding the farm—and her father—as much as possible. A few people in Ballybeg still threw her and Brian quizzical looks, but for the most part, they were left in peace.

On the Wednesday before the Christmas bazaar, Sharon was on a high after sitting the last exam of the semester. She and Brian had handed in their joint research paper on Monday, and she had a giddy feeling they'd nailed it.

Naomi was sitting at one of the tables in the small café in the Book Mark, sipping a cappuccino while Bridie and Sharon gift-wrapped a mountain of books.

She and Naomi had practiced making their wares and had a nice stockpile of divine-smelling bath products to sell on Saturday.

"I still can't believe you're going out with Brian Glenn." Naomi shook her head in wonder, making her beads jangle. "It's been, what, six weeks? That must be a record for you."

"More like nine." Sharon added a red bow to the book she was wrapping and reached for the scissors. "He's a man, I'm a woman. We like each other. End of story."

More than liked. She was in serious danger of falling in love with Brian Glenn. Assuming she wasn't already...

"Because he's a cop and you're..." Naomi trailed off, meeting Sharon's hard stare.

"A MacCarthy?" Sharon ripped the edge of the scissors against the ribbon to make it curl. "Oh, for feck's sake. Ruairí's a MacCarthy too, and no one ever assumes he's up to anything dodgy. I'm sick of people judging me because my father's an arse and my eldest brother is in prison. It's not fair. The rest of us aren't in trouble with the police."

"Not anymore, you mean," Naomi added with a grin, making Bridie snort with laughter.

"Fine." Sharon threw her arms up in a gesture of admission. "So I haven't always taken the law very seriously. But I'm older now and wiser and more aware of the consequences."

"Careful you don't turn into a paragon of virtue," Bridie said with a chuckle. "We wouldn't recognize you."

"I don't think I want to be friends with a paragon of anything," Naomi added with a shudder.

Sharon gave a bark of laughter. "I don't think there's *any* danger of that."

Her friend drained her cup and brought it to the counter. "What's the Batcave like?" she asked. "You were always keen to get a look inside."

"It's nice. He's into colorful deco and comfy furniture. I wasn't expecting that. I was sure he'd go for the minimalist look."

"I can't see you living in a minimalist environment," Naomi said slyly.

"Hey, Nomes. Don't jump the gun. We've only started going out. I'm not planning to move in with him yet."

"Ah, just wait. I predict a proposal under the mistletoe."

"Don't be daft. I don't want to get married at my age, and Brian's only twenty-five."

"Well, a kiss, then," Naomi amended. "At least one of us will see some action under the mistletoe this festive season... unless Bridie's planning to ambush the Major at the Christmas bazaar."

"I don't need to ambush him," Bridie said primly, "because I already have. I told him I was making an honest man out of him this New Year, and Major Johnson had the good sense to agree."

"What?" Sharon clapped in delight and let out a whoop. "You're marrying the Major? That's wonderful news."

An amused smirk lurked on Bridie's lips. "He and Jasper need looking after. I figure I'm the woman for the job."

"Jasper?" Naomi glanced at Sharon for guidance.

"The Major's Cavalier King Charles spaniel." Sharon stepped forward and gave her boss a hug. "I'm thrilled for you, Bridie. Congratulations."

"You're both invited to the reception, of course," her boss said. "New Year's Eve at Clonmore Castle Hotel.

Olivia is marrying Jonas on the same day, so we thought we'd make it a double celebration."

"I'll definitely be there." Sharon whipped a bottle of champagne out of the small fridge beneath the counter. "I think this calls for a toast. Just as well I picked up a bottle of bubbly on my way home from Cork."

"Don't you want to save that to have with Brian?" Bridie asked.

"He'll understand, especially when I tell him the occasion."

Bridie gave a sly smirk. "I'm assuming he'll be your plus-one to the wedding."

"I certainly hope so." Sharon poured the dancing liquid into teacups and handed them to the other women.

"Classy," said Naomi with a grin.

"Hey, I have a reputation to live down to. I can't let a soon-to-be university degree and a steady boyfriend totally cramp my style." She raised her cup. "*Sláinte*, ladies. Here's to new relationships and new beginnings."

"Have you no decent man on the horizon?" Bridie asked Naomi as she stacked the beautifully wrapped Christmas gift packages on a display table.

"No man at all, decent or otherwise." Naomi wrinkled her nose. "Men either find me exotic—how I loathe that description—or they don't want to go out with a black girl."

"Idiots," Bridie said. "All of them. You put us pale white women to shame with your gorgeous skin tone."

"Plus no one in Ireland can tell the difference between black and mixed race. If you have any bit of *different* in you, that's the part people focus on."

"Don't mind them, Nomes." Sharon reached across to give her a hug. "You need a man with discernment. Unfortunately they're few and far between—especially in Ballybeg. I think Bridie and I nabbed the only two."

"Right, girls. I'm off to the hairdresser." Bridie drained her cup of bubbly and retrieved her handbag from under the counter. "You'll be all right to close up on your own, Sharon?"

"No problem." Sharon grinned at her employer. "What color are you going for this time?"

"I'm thinking of a red rinse for the festive season," Bridie said expansively. "Gavin and Fiona are bringing Wiggly Poo round for Christmas dinner. After last year's fiasco, I don't want to risk getting a tree, so I figured I'd better decorate myself."

Sharon was still laughing when her boss left the shop. "Okay," she said, turning to her friend. "What's up with you today, Naomi? You've been hovering for the past thirty minutes as if you want to talk to me about something."

Her friend grimaced. "You don't miss a trick."

"Nope. And if you want a chat, now's your chance. A customer could arrive at any moment."

"Right." Naomi hesitated and drew in a deep breath. "It's about us renting the flat upstairs."

"Yeah?" A sense of foreboding made Sharon's stomach churn.

"My sister keeps saying she can pull a few strings and get me a job at her company in Dublin."

Sharon blinked, then released an internal sigh. "And you want to take her up on the offer. If you have any sense, you will."

"I promised you we'd get a flat together." Naomi fiddled with one of her dangly earrings. "I don't want to let you down."

"So that's why you've been in an odd mood lately." Sharon moved forward to touch her friend's arm. "Seriously, Naomi. Do you really think I'd hold you back from the chance of a fresh start?"

"No, that's just it." Naomi bit her lip. "I knew you'd encourage me to take her up on the offer. If I do, where does that leave you? You can't afford to rent the flat upstairs on your own, and I don't want you taking on extra hours in your final year in an effort to escape your father."

"I'm a survivor. Always have been. Yeah, I'd like to leave the farm and my father's odious presence, but that's my problem, not yours. I can always ask Brian if I can study at his place more often. I'm there a couple of days a week as it is."

All this was true. It didn't mitigate the disappointment that was deflating her mood. She'd let herself believe the flat upstairs was a done deal. How would Brian react if she started spending even more time at his house? And she didn't want to take advantage of him by overstaying her welcome at his house. She took a deep breath and turned to her friend. "Call Jill today and tell her you'll take that job. It'll do you good to get out of Ballybeg."

"Are you sure?"

"Of course I'm sure. What kind of friend would hold you back from an opportunity this good?"

"You're the best." Naomi gave her a hug. "Promise you'll visit me in the Big Smoke?"

"I'll visit so often you'll be sick of the sight of me." Sharon plastered a smile on her face, determined to stem the gnawing doubts and worries that were threatening to derail her day.

CHAPTER TEN

....

O n the day of the Christmas bazaar, Brian strolled
into Ballybeg's town hall wearing a heavy
overcoat and a huge grin. Although the
temperature had plummeted over the past few days,
nothing could chill his good mood.

He spotted Sharon and Naomi's stand over in a
corner by an enormous Christmas tree and made a
beeline for it.

Sharon was bagging an array of colored bath
products for a customer. Her green pullover was snug-
fitting and traffic light bright. His gaze trailed down her
curves to the studded leather platform heels. The sight
made him chuckle. She had the zaniest taste in clothes,
but she could pull off even the most outlandish of
outfits.

She glanced up at his approach, and a wide smile
suffused her face. "Well, hey, you! Come to make sure
there's no illegal substances lurking in the bath salts?"

He rounded the stand and kissed her on the lips.
"Shockingly, no. I have news. I went by the psychology
department's notice board this morning."

She sucked in a breath, and her skin turned chalky
white. "And?"

"And... our research project was the best in the class."

She whooped with delight. "Seriously?"

"Seriously. We got first class honors."

She slumped against his chest, laughing. "I've never done this well on any test or paper before. It must be your influence."

"I think it bodes well for the rest of your grades this semester. You've worked really hard."

Crazy though it might sound, he was even happier for her sake than he was for his own. She'd put so much work into the project, and she tended to doubt herself when it came to her academic ability. With a bit of luck, this success would boost her confidence.

He tugged her ponytail playfully. "I'd love to drag you away from here right now and celebrate."

"I can't abandon the stand. We're selling gangbusters here, aren't we, Nomes?"

Naomi was flicking through the cash box, doing a quick count. "We've already doubled what we spent on ingredients. I have to hand it to you, Sharon. You were right."

Brian slipped his hand around Sharon's. "Much as I'd love to hang here with you, I'd better do the rounds. I'm not officially on duty today, but I promised Seán I'd stop by to see if he needed help."

"Aren't you going to drag your girlfriend under the mistletoe?" Naomi demanded, pointing toward the huge boughs suspended over the entrance.

"No dragging required," Sharon said, teasing his stubble. "I'd be a willing participant."

"Then I'll make sure to maneuver you under those boughs later." And he'd do so with pleasure. These past couple of months had been the best in his life. He walked with a new spring to his step, and a smile was never far from his lips.

He dropped a final kiss on her cheek and sauntered off in the direction of the punch stand, where Seán was chatting to one of the town councilors. He waved when he spotted Brian.

"How's it going?" Brian asked.

"Pretty quiet so far." Seán frowned. "I have a feeling John-Joe Fitzgerald and Buck MacCarthy are up to some sort of mischief. They're acting shifty."

"Isn't acting shifty their usual modus operandi?"

"Yeah, but I could have sworn I saw Pat Dolan slip John-Joe a fifty earlier."

Brian shrugged. "No crime in giving someone money."

"No. However, I doubt Dolan was giving him a Christmas present. That pair are up to something. I just can't put my finger on what."

"I'll keep an eye on them over Christmas. They're always in and out of Buck's garden shed. I've no idea what they're up to in there, and I can hardly go barging in without a warrant."

Seán grimaced. "Unfortunately, no."

"Do you need me to patrol the building?"

"Ah, no. Unless John-Joe and Buck cause a riot, I'll be fine on my own."

"In that case, I'll take some punch over to Sharon and Naomi."

He strode back across the hall, reaching the bath product stand at the same instant that Colm MacCarthy burst into the building.

***

Da scanned the crowd—eyes blazing, nostrils flaring. Sharon's stomach lodged in her throat. *Ah, feck.* Had he discovered she was seeing Brian? While she hadn't made a secret of their relationship, she hadn't gone out of her way to inform her father. It wasn't like they communicated, for heaven's sake. Whenever she had the misfortune to run into him at the house, he demanded clean laundry and farm chores. She had no problem with the latter. She also had no issue with contributing to household bills. Doing his laundry was another matter.

Her father marched over to the stand. "What's this I hear about you going out with that cop?"

She'd known full well that his reaction to the news his daughter was dating a policeman would be ferocious, but she hadn't expected him to freak out during the bazaar. Talk about bad timing. Behind Colm's greasy gray head, potential customers were retracing their steps, and Naomi had retreated to the far end of their stand.

Sharon crossed her arms and fixed her father with a belligerent stare. "Here to buy bath products, Da? I recommend something containing ylang-ylang. It has a sedative effect."

He bared his nicotine-stained teeth in a snarl. "I heard a rumor weeks ago about you and that fuckwit, Brian Glenn. I thought it was nonsense, but your uncle Buck tells me you're in and out of Glenn's house at all hours of the night."

"Buck should mind his own business and clean his house for a change. There's a weird smell wafting out of that place every time I walk past."

Her father's eyes widened a fraction, then narrowed to serpentine slits. "Forget about Buck."

"Gladly. *You* brought him up."

Colm's jaw flexed. "Is it true about you and Glenn?"

"Yeah. So what? I'm twenty-one, Da. Old enough to spend time with whomever I choose."

"Not while you're living under my roof. No daughter of mine is going out with a cop."

"This one is, so you'd better get used to the idea."

He let out a low growl like an animal about to go on the attack. "I want you out of my house by tonight. You're no longer welcome at the farm."

His words hit her like a lash. She'd expected anger. She'd expected insults. She hadn't expected to be evicted with two hours' notice.

Brian shoved through the curious crowd and deposited two plastic cups of punch on the table.

At the sight of him, Colm's features contorted in a spasm of rage.

"Don't even start, MacCarthy." Brian's northern lilt deepened into a growl. "You're a pig and a crap excuse for a father. If you don't want Sharon in your house, she's welcome in mine."

Sharon started. "What? That's very good of you, but—

He put a hand on her arm and looked at her earnestly. "It's no problem. You can stay with me until you move into your new flat."

The flat... oh, crap. Beside her, she heard Naomi's sharp intake of breath.

"Ah, thanks, Brian," she said hastily. "That would be great. I'll be out of your hair after Christmas."

"If you want her Glenn, take her." Da jutted a finger at Sharon. "I'll be at the pub until late. I want your crap gone by the time I get back."

And with that charming parting shot, Sharon's father stomped into the crowd.

Brian glared daggers into Colm's retreating back. "That man is a bastard."

"He's always been a nasty piece of work," Naomi said. "Why don't you head out to the farm now? I can pack up the stand."

"Are you sure? I don't want to leave you in the lurch."

"You won't be. Our bath products were such a success that there's hardly anything left to pack up." Naomi threw Sharon her winter jacket. "Go on," she said with a loaded look, "I'm sure you and Brian have stuff to talk about."

Like the fallen-through flatshare that she'd postponed mentioning. Yeah, she should have told him about that three days ago, but she didn't want him to feel obliged to offer her a room in his house. She absolutely did not want him to think she was taking advantage of his good nature. Accepting his hospitality for a couple of weeks was one thing, but longer than that wouldn't be fair.

Coaxing her features into a cheerful expression, she shrugged on her coat and wrapped her scarf around her neck. "Talk to you later, Nomes."

Brian linked his arm through hers. It felt good to walk through the crowd as a couple. It felt right.

"You okay?" he asked when they were outside the town hall.

"No, but I will be." Her father's fury had shaken her more than she'd expected. "I'd say his Christmas dinner is screwed now that he's evicted the family chef. Neither Mickey nor Shea can cook."

Brian gave a low laugh and took his car key from his coat pocket. "I take it none of your other siblings are planning to invite him round for the festive season?"

"Hell, no. To be frank, I'm dreading Christmas." Sharon dug her hands into her pockets.

"Because it'll be the first one without you mother?" he asked gently.

"Yeah, but it's not just that. I feel like all the siblings I get on with are abandoning me, even though I realize I'm being irrational. Ruairí and Jayme are going to America to spend time with her family before their baby is born. Marcella's going to a hotel with her girlfriend. Sinéad and her kids are invited to her in-laws'. Until Da's little outburst, I was scheduled to cook for him,

Shea, and Mikey. Not that I regret missing out on that experience. It would have gone like last Christmas. Ma was too sick to cook, so I took over. Then the men all bitched about my lack of culinary skills and left me to wash up while they passed out in front of the telly."

"Maybe they'll appreciate the effort you made while they're burning the turkey this year." Brian stroked her cheek, sending pings of awareness skittering across her skin. "You're not their slave, Sharon. We'll cook our own Christmas dinner."

She blinked in confusion. "Wait... aren't you going to Donegal to be with your family?"

"No can do. I'm on duty while Seán is in Dublin. I can't leave Ballybeg until he gets back on the twenty-seventh."

"Oh." Her voice held hope. "So you'd have been all on your own?"

"Just me and a microwave dinner from Marks and Spencer." He pressed the automatic lock on his car and opened the passenger door. "I'm delighted to have your company over Christmas."

She slid her hands beneath his coat. "I'd love to spend the holiday with you, but I draw the line at a microwave dinner. A turkey for two is a bit much. How about ham, spuds, and brussels sprouts?"

"Sounds perfect. We can toast our academic success and your new flat. Come January, you'll be escaping your father for good, not just for Christmas."

Her smile wavered and she averted her gaze.

"What's wrong? Didn't you and Naomi earn the money you'd been hoping for?"

"We did."

He raised a questioning eyebrow. "But?"

"But nothing." She kissed him on the cheek and got into the car. "Let's get going before we freeze."

....

CHAPTER ELEVEN

While neither of them would earn a Michelin star, their Christmas dinner had turned out surprisingly well.

Sharon reached for the wine bottle and topped up their wine glasses. "Nice job, Garda Glenn. We rock at coproductions."

"Yeah, we do." Brian held up a hand to stop her from filling his glass to the brim. "I'm on call, remember?"

"What's going to happen in Ballybeg on Christmas Day?" she asked, taking a generous swig from her glass. "Even my crazy relatives tend to be too full to do more than pass out in front of the telly."

He twisted his mouth into a half smile. "You'd be surprised. Christmas brings out the worst in families. We're usually called out on one or two domestics."

"Can't the reserve police handle it on their own?"

"If it's nothing serious, yes. We have a part-timer and two reservists on duty today, with me at the ready if needed."

She put her elbows on the table and leaned forward, relishing the sight of his dilating pupils when he admired her exposed cleavage. Having the power to turn him on was a powerful aphrodisiac. "Who knew Ballybeg needed so much policing? Apart from the murder over the summer, not much happens around here. Don't you long for a bit more action?"

Brian shook his head. "Not me. I like the pace of policing Ballybeg. Seán's the one keen for more action."

"Bridie said he used to be a detective. How does a Dublin detective end up in a place like Ballybeg?"

Brian shrugged. "I don't know the particulars, and I don't ask. It's none of my business. I assume he was demoted for some reason or other. Whatever happened, he's a damn good cop, but definitely not cut out for a country posting."

"And you are?" she teased.

"I think so," he replied after giving it some consideration. "For me, this job is all about the people. I like going out on patrol. I don't want to be stuck in an office all day, even one with a nonleaking roof and a better computer. If my degree leads to a promotion, I hope it'll be around here or in Cork City."

"Thanks again for letting me stay. I hope my gear isn't crowding you out of your house."

"No problem. It's been a pleasure having you here."

She toyed with his knee under the table. "In more ways than one, I hope."

He wagged a finger. "Sharon, Sharon. Always with the sexual innuendoes."

"Ah, go on. You know you love it."

"I know I love—" He broke off and flushed to the tips of his ears.

Sharon's heart pounded against her ribs. Had he been going to say he loved her? If anyone had told her at this time a year ago that she'd be anxiously waiting for a guy to declare his love for her, she'd have busted a rib laughing. Yet here she was, fingers tense around the stem of her wine glass, anxiously waiting for Brian to utter those three words.

His Adam's apple bobbed. He took a swig from his water glass. Tension hung in the air, taut as a rubber band.

Sharon broke the silence. "There's something I need to tell you. I've been putting off saying it because I was afraid you'd think I was trying to take advantage of you."

A muscle flexed in his cheek. "Go on."

"It's about the flat Naomi and I were going to rent from Bridie. It's not happening."

His pale blue eyes flew upward. "What? I thought you had enough money to pay the rental deposit."

"I do, but I can't afford to pay the rent on my own now that Naomi is moving to Dublin."

"Why didn't you mention this before?"

"I wanted to sort out an alternative solution for the New Year. I think I've found one. A girl in one of my psychology classes is moving in with her boyfriend. I might be able to take over her room on campus."

He fixed her with one of his knowing looks. "Do you want to live in a dorm during your final semester?"

She shrugged. "It'll be fine. I'll be spending most of my time in the library anyway. So," she said, keen to steer the conversation in a more pleasant direction, "if you're in danger of being summoned to work at any moment, why don't we defer the Christmas cake until later and go upstairs? I still have to give you your Christmas present."

"Sounds very naughty." His slow-burn smile made her want to reach across and kiss him.

"Oh, it is." She leaned forward to nibble his earlobe. "But I think you'll like it."

"What about the dishes?"

"Leave them. I don't want to waste time."

Upstairs in Brian's bedroom, Sharon kicked the door closed. "I went all out for the festive season."

She pulled her top over her head to reveal a sheer red bra with little silk ribbons barely holding the material together over the nipple area.

Brian whistled in appreciation. "Very nice."

"And, of course, I bought matching knickers." She slid her skirt over her hips, watching his pupils dilate when he caught sight of the thong.

He stepped forward and ran a finger over her hip and unraveled one of the ribbons holding her thong together. "I'm going to have fun getting you out of that."

Her breathing turned shallow. "I'm going to have fun letting you."

He lowered her onto the bed and applied himself to the task of undoing all her ribbons. "You certainly wrapped this package very nicely," he murmured, "but I'm looking forward to exploring its contents."

When he freed a nipple from its gauzy confines and claimed it with his mouth, Sharon arched her back and groaned. "Oh, yes," she sighed. "I think I'm going to enjoy your present just as much as you will."

She was relaxing back into the pillows when a sudden blast ripped through her eardrums and rattled the windows in their frames.

CHAPTER TWELVE

....

"What the hell?" Brian leaped off the bed and ran to the window. "Jaysus, Sharon. Your uncle's shed is on fire." He snatched his mobile phone from the nightstand and hit the button for the emergency services while he threw on a pair of jeans. Pulling on a shirt, he raced down the stairs and out the door. "Stay here," he yelled. "It might be dangerous."

As he pounded down the pavement, it occurred to him that those words were more likely to send Sharon after him than persuade her to stay inside.

Out on the street, a crowd was gathering. Brian ran the length of a few houses until he stopped outside Buck MacCarthy's shabby dwelling. It was in desperate need of a fresh coat of paint, and the roof was missing more than a few slates.

He scaled the wooden gate at the side of the house that separated the front from the back garden and gasped at the sight before him.

Buck's shed was engulfed in a fiery ball. The man himself and his partner in crime, John-Joe Fitzgerald, stood on the grass, singed and filthy but otherwise unharmed. It would take an atomic bomb to fell that pair, Brian thought grimly.

"What the hell happened?" he yelled at them over the roar of the flames. He ran to the garden tap and switched on the hose. Aiming it at the shed, he angled himself close to the exit in case a quick getaway was called for. "Don't loiter, lads. Start filling buckets of water."

Thankfully Buck and John-Joe's halfhearted attempts at hurling water on the flames weren't essential. Even before they heard the sirens of the fire brigade approaching in the distance, it was clear that Brian and the hose were winning the battle against the flames.

When the last burning piece of wood had been extinguished, he stood back and wiped the sweat from his brow. "What the hell was in that shed?"

Buck and John-Joe shuffled on the spot, shooting guilty glances at one another.

"Out with it," he demanded. "We'll find out no matter what."

After hacking phlegm, John-Joe found his voice. "Just a spot of the old *poitín*."

"You eejits were making *moonshine* in Buck's garden shed? Buck's *wooden* garden shed?"

Again, the guilty shuffle and shifty glances. "It seemed like a good idea at the time," Buck muttered. "We didn't think."

"When do you ever think?" Brian tossed the hose on the grass in disgust. "So that's what you were up to at the Christmas bazaar. Did you pass any of the stuff on to customers?"

"A few," muttered John-Joe. "Pat Dolan, Colm MacCarthy, and some others."

"You'd better give me their names so I can check if they're still breathing. I don't trust the pair of you not to make a lethal concoction."

The firefighters were trooping in now, Sharon hot on their heels. "Oh my goodness," she exclaimed, running to his side and hurling herself into his arms. "Are you all right?"

"I'm fine," he said, returning her embrace, "but I'm going to get you filthy."

"Shag that. It'll wash off. When I saw the flames above the garden and knew you'd gone in there, I was terrified."

"Well, Garda Glenn," came the gruff voice of the fire chief. "Looks like you've done our job for us. Any idea what caused the fire?"

"Apparently, these fools were making *poitín*." Brian shot a look of disgust at the perpetrators of the catastrophe.

"Good God." The fire chief looked suitably appalled at the notion of John-Joe and Buck meddling with distilling equipment. "It's a wonder the whole street didn't burn to the ground."

Two reserve policemen trooped into the garden and regarded the scene with appropriate horror.

"McGarry. Doyle. Help me get this pair of miscreants down the station. We need statements."

"Right-oh, sir." The two reserves dragged a by-now-subdued Buck and John-Joe out the gate and into the waiting vehicle.

Brian dropped a kiss on Sharon's forehead, leaving a sooty smudge that was too adorable to erase. "I'll see you later."

She clung to his arm. "Will you be long?"

"Shouldn't be too long. They're too shaken up to be uncooperative."

She flashed him a naughty grin. "I'll be waiting."

***

Four hours later, Brian opened his front door. "Sharon? I'm home. Can you come here for a sec?"

She appeared at the top of the stairs, clad in a negligee, spiky heels, and nothing else.

He gave a low whistle. "Hey, gorgeous. Come here and stand under this yoke before my arm goes numb holding it over my head."

"Is that mistletoe?" she asked, squinting down at him.

"It is indeed. I nicked it from the station's lobby. We were supposed to kiss under the mistletoe at the Christmas bazaar, remember?"

"Only my father came blustering in and derailed our plan." Taking the steps carefully on her towering heels, Sharon descended to the hallway.

"Well, Garda Glenn, having been rudely interrupted earlier today, I hope you intend to make it up to me."

"Why don't I start by giving you that kiss?"

He leaned down and captured her mouth with his. Her lips were soft and supple and she tasted of red wine and peppermint toothpaste.

"Was that worth waiting for?" he asked when he released her.

"More than worth it." She tugged the mistletoe out of his hand. "You can put your arm down now."

"Before we go upstairs, there's something I want to say to you." He gazed into her warm brown orbs. "I love you, Sharon MacCarthy. I've been crazy about you for years, but I never thought it would work between us. These past couple of months have proven me wrong in the best possible way."

Her eyes grew moist, and she gave him a wobbly smile. "I love you too, Brian Glenn. And it scares me. I don't want to screw this up. I keep thinking you'll come to your senses because I'm so—"

"So uniquely you? That's exactly what I love about you." He pulled her into his arms and inhaled the sweet scent of her shampoo. "I don't want you living on campus, in a flat with Naomi, or anywhere that's not here. Will you move in with me?"

"Officially?" she said with a laugh. "As opposed to having all my stuff crammed into your guest room and taking up half your bedroom wardrobe?"

"More than half." He tweaked her nose. "Don't think I didn't notice you sneak those dresses onto my hangers."

"Busted."

"So will you come and live with me?"

Her sunny smile could melt an iceberg. "Of course I will, you eejit. You'll never get rid of me."

He took her hand and tugged her toward the stairs. "I can't imagine I'll ever want to."

EPILOGUE

....

THREE YEARS LATER

Excerpt from the *Ballybeg Chronicle*

The staff at the *Ballybeg Chronicle* wish to extend their heartfelt congratulations to local police sergeant, Brian Glenn, son of James and Geraldine Glenn (Cloghan, Co. Donegal), on his marriage last Saturday to child psychologist Sharon MacCarthy, daughter of Colm and the late Molly MacCarthy (Ballybeg). The wedding ceremony took place in St. Mary's Church, with the reception held at Clonmore Castle Hotel. The bride wore a gown of fuchsia silk and was attended by two bridesmaids (Naomi Bekele and Marcella MacCarthy) and four flower girls (Sally Glenn, Stacey O'Driscoll, Blánaid O'Driscoll, and Lucy MacCarthy). Best man was Detective Inspector Seán Mackey. After a honeymoon on the island of Santorini, Greece, the couple will reside in Ballybeg.

THANK YOU!

....

Thanks for reading *Love and Mistletoe*. I hope you enjoyed it!

Love and Mistletoe is the fourth book in the Ballybeg series. All the stories are designed to stand alone—Happy Ever Afters guaranteed! However, you might prefer to read them in order of publication to follow the development of the secondary characters and happenings in the town.

To find out what's next, or to sign up to my new release mailing list, check out my author website at:

http://zarakeane.com

You can also turn the page to read a blurb *Love and Leprechauns* (Ballybeg, #3).

LOVE AND LEPRECHAUNS

(BALLYBEG, #3)

....

Tattooed in Tipperary...
Olivia Gant is determined to escape her abusive husband and build a new life. Only desperation drives her to rent business premises from Jonas O'Mahony, the man who tattooed her behind and broke her heart. Can she maintain a haughty distance?

Jonas is a struggling single father. The last person he wants next door is the beautiful-but-infuriating Olivia. A childcare crisis forces him to strike a bargain with her: the lease to the cottage in return for babysitting. Can he resist her allures?

...True Love in Ballybeg.
When Olivia's ex is clobbered to death with a garden gnome, the fickle finger of suspicion points to Olivia and Jonas. Can they prove their innocence, or is their happily ever after doomed?

OUT NOW!

OTHER BOOKS BY ZARA

....

1. *Love and Shenanigans* (novel)
2. *Love and Blarney* (novella)
3. *Love and Leprechauns* (novel)
4. *Love and Mistletoe* (novella)
5. *Love and Shamrocks* (novel) Coming 2015

ACKNOWLEDGEMENTS

Love and Mistletoe was one of those rare stories that seemed to write itself. Nevertheless, a number of people helped me to polish it before publication.

Many thanks are due to my wonderful critique partner, Magdalen Braden, for her insightful comments; to Rhonda Helms, editor extraordinaire, for working her magic on the manuscript; to Trish Slattery and April Weigele for beta reading the final draft; and to Anne and Linda at Victory Editing for the thorough proofread.

Finally, thank you to my readers for supporting the Ballybeg series. I wish you a wonderful festive season and a Happy New Year!

ABOUT ZARA KEANE

....

Zara Keane grew up in Dublin, Ireland, but spent her summers in a small town very similar to the fictitious Ballybeg.

She currently lives in Switzerland with her family. When she's not writing or wrestling small people, she drinks far too much coffee, and tries—with occasional success —to resist the siren call of Swiss chocolate.

zarakeane.com

28011961R00063

Printed in Great Britain
by Amazon